MASTER THIEF OF HELL

Who are his foes? All who would despise him or love the
Lord of Bats: Smage of the Jackass Ears, the Colonel
Who Never Died, the Borshin, and Quazer, winner of the
Hellgames and abductor of the voluptuous Evene. One
by one, Shadowjack would seek them out and have his
revenge, building his power as he goes. And once his
vengeance is obtained, he would come to terms with all
others who are against him, he would unite the World
of High Dudgeon, destroy the Land of Filth, and bring
peace to the Shadowguard. But to accomplish all, Jack
of Shadows must find Kolwynia, the Key That Was
Lost. . . .

JACK OF SHADOWS

JACK
OF
SHADOWS

ROGER ZELAZNY

A SIGNET BOOK

NEW AMERICAN LIBRARY

A DIVISION OF PENGUIN BOOKS USA INC.

Some there be that shadows kiss,
Such have but a shadow's bliss.

THE MERCHANT OF VENICE

NAL BOOKS ARE AVAILABLE AT QUANTITY DISCOUNTS WHEN
USED TO PROMOTE PRODUCTS OR SERVICES. FOR INFORMATION
PLEASE WRITE TO PREMIUM MARKETING DIVISION, NEW AMERI-
CAN LIBRARY, 1633 BROADWAY, NEW YORK, NEW YORK 10019.

SIGNET TRADEMARK REG. U.S. PAT. OFF. AND FOREIGN COUNTRIES
REGISTERED TRADEMARK—MARCA REGISTRADA
HECHO EN DRESDEN, TN

SIGNET, SIGNET CLASSIC, MENTOR, ONYX, PLUME, MERIDIAN
and NAL BOOKS are published by New American Library,
a division of Penguin Books USA Inc.,
1633 Broadway, New York, New York 10019

First Printing, August, 1972

10   11   12   13   14   15   16

PRINTED IN THE UNITED STATES OF AMERICA

Foreword

PEOPLE SOMETIMES ASK me whether the title
Jack of Shadows was intended to sound like a
description of a playing card used in some ar-
cane game, as well as representing my protagonist's name and a matter of geography. Answer:
Yes. I've long been fascinated by odd decks of
cards, and I had an extensive collection of them
at one time.

"Ha!" they usually respond on hearing this
admission. "Then this business about the cards
and the reference to shadows ties this story in at
some subterranean psychological level with your
Amber books, right?"

Well, no. The last time I was down in the
catacombs I couldn't locate any connection. I
was simply attracted by the imagery. On the
other hand, nobody ever asked me, "Why Jack?"

I could have answered that one: Jack Vance.

In this, my tenth book, I'd decided to try for something on the order of those rare and exotic settings I admired so much in so many of Jack Vance's stories. It seemed only fair then, once I'd worked things out, to find a title with "Jack" in it as a private bit of homage publicly displayed. Now you all know.

I suppose the inferences concerning a relationship to Amber could have been strengthened, though, by the fact that this book came out between the publication of *Nine Princes in Amber* and *The Guns of Avalon*, the first two books in that series—proximity breeding speculation and like that.

But while the setting may owe something to Jack Vance, the character doesn't. I took my opening quotation from *The Merchant of Venice* only because it seemed so apt once I'd pried it free of its context. The Shakespearean work to which I actually do owe a debt here came along about eight years after *Merchant*. I refer to *Macbeth*. True, Birnam Wood does not come against Jack, and the play contains no quote I wanted to uproot and employ here. But Jack's character undergoes an interesting progression, which owes something to Shakespeare's portrait of the bloody Scot. I don't care to say anything more about it, though, because I feel that introductory pieces should not spoil story lines. Someone named J. I. M. Stewart almost ruined *Vanity Fair* for me that way years ago.

This was not one of my experimental books, such as *Creatures of Light and Darkness, Doorways in the Sand, Bridge of Ashes, Roadmarks* or *Eye of Cat*. Those are the five wherein I worked out lots of techniques I used in many of the others. This was a more workmanlike job in that I knew exactly what I wanted to do and how to do it, with the protagonist—as usual—indicating the direction. Of the five, only *Creatures of Light and Darkness* preceded *Jack of Shadows*. Looking back upon *Jack* in this light, I do feel that I might have gained a certain facility there for the brief, impressionistic description of the exotic which could have carried over into both *Nine Princes* and *Jack*. And maybe not. But if it owes it anything, that's it.

It is interesting to me, too, in looking at a story across the years this way, to see it in terms of what came after as well as what preceded it. I do feel that the shadow of Jack fell upon the protagonist of *Today We Choose Faces*. Also, there is something of Jack's sardonic attitude as well as his caution in the later tales of Dilvish the Damned—another wrongfully punished man whose character was twisted by the act.

I have also been asked several times whether the name that Jack assumes Dayside—Jonathan Shade—owes anything to the character of that name in Nabokov's *Pale Fire*. Sorry. While I do enjoy playing an occasional literary puzzle game, I wrote *Jack of Shadows before* I came to PALE FIRE.

And yes, I did once do a short graphic prequel to this book ("Shadowjack") in collaboration with artist Gray Morrow, in *The Illustrated Roger Zelazny*. And no, nothing in that story is essential to the understanding or enjoyment of this one. It is a minor piece, and totally independent.

So this is the story that Jack built—with a little help from me on the paperwork. Picture him if you will as a figure on a playing card. Make it a Tarot. Maybe the Broken Tower . . .

1

IT HAPPENED WHEN Jack whose name is spoken in shadow went to Iglés, in the Twilight Lands, to visit the Hellgames. It was there that he was observed while considering the situation of the Hellflame.

The Hellflame was a slim urn of silvery fires, gracefully wrought and containing a fist-sized ruby at the uppermost tips of its blazing fingers. These held it in an unbreakable grip, and the gemstone glimmered coolly despite them.

Now, the Hellflame was on display for all to regard, but the fact that Jack was seen looking at it was cause for much consternation. Newly arrived in Iglés, he was first noticed while passing amid lanterns, in line with the other on-lookers, who were moving through the open-sided display pavilion. He was recognized by Smage and

Quazer, who had left their places of power to
come to compete for the trophy. They immediately moved to report him to the Games Master.

Smage shifted his weight from foot to foot
and tugged at his mustache until the tears rose
in his squarish eyes and he began to blink. He
stared up at his giant companion Quazer—hair,
eyes, flesh all of a uniform gray—rather than
regard the colorful bulk of Benoni, the Games
Master, whose will was law in this place.

"What do you two want?" he inquired.

Smage continued to stare and blink until
Quazer finally spoke in his flute-like fashion.

"We have information for you," he said.

"I hear you. Tell it," replied Benoni.

"We have recognized one whose presence
here should be cause for some concern."

"Who?"

"We must move near to a light before I may
tell you."

The Games Master twisted his head on his
bulging neck, and his amber eyes flashed as he
glared first at the one, then at the other.

"If this is some sort of prank—" he began.

"It is not," said Quazer unflinchingly.

"Very well, then. Follow me." He sighed;
and with a swirl of his orange and green cloak,
he turned and headed toward a brightly illumi-
nated tent.

Inside, he faced them once again. "Is this
bright enough for you?"

Quazer looked about. "Yes," he said. "He will not overhear us."

"Who are you talking about?" asked the Games Master.

"Do you know of one called Jack, who always hears his name if it is spoken in shadows?"

"Jack of Shadows? The thief?—Yes, I've heard stories."

"That is why we wished to speak with you in a brightly lit place. He is here. Smage and I saw him only a few minutes ago. He was studying the Hellflame."

"Oh my!" The Games Master's eyes were wide and his mouth remained open after the exclamation. "He'll steal it!" he said.

Smage stopped touching his mustache long enough to nod several times. ". . . And we're here to try to win it," he blurted. "We can't if it is stolen."

"He must be stopped," said the Games Master. "What do you think I should do?"

"Your will is the law here," said Quazer.

"True . . . Perhaps I should confine him to some lock-up for the duration of the Games."

"In that case," said Quazer, "make certain that there are no shadows in the place where he is captured or in the place where he is to be confined. He is said to be exceedingly difficult to contain—especially in the presence of shadows."

"But there are shadows all over the place!"

"Yes. That is the main difficulty in keeping him prisoner."

"Then either brilliant lights or total darkness would seem to be the answer."

"But unless all the lights are set at perfect angles," said Quazer, "and inaccessible, he will be able to create shadows with which to work. And in darkness, if he can strike but just the smallest light, there will be shadows."

"What strength does he derive from shadows?"

"I know of no one who knows for certain."

"He is a darksider, then? Not human?"

"Some say twilight, but close to the dark—where there are always shadows."

"In that case, a trip to the Dung Pits of Glyve might be in order."

"Cruel," said Smage, and he chuckled.

"Come point him out to me," said the Games Master.

They departed from the tent. The sky was gray overhead, changing to silver in the east and black in the west. Stars dotted the darkness above a row of stalagmitical mountains. There were no clouds.

They moved along the torchlit way that crossed the compound, heading toward the pavilion of the Hellflame. There was a flicker of lightning in the west, near, it seemed, to that place on the boundary where the shrines of the helpless gods stood.

As they neared the open side of the pavilion, Quazer touched Benoni's arm and nodded. The Games Master followed the direction of his gesture with his eyes to where a tall, thin man stood leaning against a tent pole. His hair was black, his complexion swarthy, his features somewhat aquiline. He wore gray garments, and a black cloak was draped over his right shoulder. He smoked some darkside weed rolled into a tube, and its smoke was blue in the torchlight.

·   For a moment Benoni studied him, sensing that feeling men know when confronting a creature born, not of woman but of an unknown darkstroke, in that place men shunned.

He swallowed once, then said, "All right. You may go now."

"We would like to help—" Quazer began.

"You may go now!"

He watched them depart and then muttered, "Trust one of them to betray another."

.   He went to collect his guard force and several dozen bright lanterns.

Jack accompanied the arresting party without offering resistance or argument. Surrounded by a party of armed men and caught at the center of a circle of light, he nodded slowly and followed their instructions, not saying a word all the while.

They conducted him to the Games Master's brightly lighted tent. He was pushed before the table at which Benoni sat. The guards moved to surround him once more with their lanterns and shadow-destroying mirrors.

"Your name is Jack," said the Games Master.

"I don't deny it."

Benoni stared into the man's dark eyes. They did not waver. The man did not blink them at all.

". . . And you are sometimes called Jack of Shadows." There was silence. "Well?"

"A man may be called many things," Jack replied.

Benoni looked away. "Bring them in," he said to one of the guards.

The guard departed, and moments later he returned with Smage and Quazer. Jack flicked a glance in their direction but remained expressionless.

"Do you know this man?" Benoni inquired.

"Yes," they said in unison.

"But you are wrong in calling him a man," Quazer continued, "for he is a darksider."

"Name him."

"He is called Jack of Shadows."

The Games Master smiled.

"It is true that a man may be called many things," he said, "but in your case there seems to be considerable agreement. —I am Benoni, Master of the Hellgames, and you are Jack of Shadows, the thief. I'd wager you are here to steal the Hellflame." There was silence again. ". . . You need not deny it or affirm it," he continued. "Your presence is ample indication of your intentions."

"I might have come to compete in the games," Jack ventured.

Benoni laughed.

"Of course! Of course!" he said, swabbing away a tear with his sleeve. "Only there is no larceny event, so we lack a category in which you may compete."

"You prejudge me—and that is unfair," said Jack. "Even if I am he who you have named, I have done nothing to give offense."

"—Yet," said Benoni. "The Hellflame is indeed a lovely object, is it not?"

Jack's eyes seemed to brighten for an instant, as his mouth twitched toward an unwilling smile.

"Most would agree on that point," he said quickly.

"And you came here to win it—in your own fashion. You are known as a most monstrous thief, darksider."

"Does that rule out my being an honest spectator at a public event?"

"When the Hellflame is involved—yes. It is priceless, and both lightsiders and darksiders lust after it. As Games Master, I cannot countenance your presence anywhere near it."

"That is the trouble with bad reputations," said Jack. "No matter what you do, you are always suspect."

"Enough! *Did* you come to steal it?"

"Only a fool would say yes."

"Then it is impossible to get an honest answer from you."

"If by 'honest answer' you mean for me to say what you want me to say, whether or not it is true, then I would say that you are correct."

"Bind his hands behind his back," said Benoni.

This was done. "How many lives do you have, darksider?" the Games Master asked.

Jack did not reply.

"Come, come now! Everyone knows that darksiders have more than one life. How many have you?"

"I don't like the sound of this," said Jack.

"It is not as if you would be dead forever."

"It is a long way back from the Dung Pits of Glyve at the Western Pole of the world, and one must walk. It sometimes takes years to constitute a new body."

"Then you've been there before?"

"Yes," said Jack, testing his bonds, "and I'd rather not have to do it again."

"Then you admit that you have at least one more life. Good! In that case, I feel no compunction in ordering your immediate execution—"

"Wait!" said Jack, tossing his head and showing his teeth. "This is ridiculous, since I have done nothing. But forget that. Whether or not I came here to steal the Hellflame, I am obviously

16

in no position to do it now. Release me, and I will voluntarily exile myself for the duration of the Hellgames. I will not enter Twilight at all, but will remain in Darkness."

"What assurance have I of this?"

"My word."

Benoni laughed again.

"The word of a darksider who is a piece of criminal folklore?" he finally said. "No, Jack. I see no way to assure the safety of the trophy but by your death. As it is within my power to order it, I do so.—Scribe! Let it be written that at this hour I have judged and ordered this thing."

A ring-bearded hunchback, whose squint made lines on a face as brittle as the parchment he took up, flourished a quill and began to write.

Jack drew himself to his full height and fixed the Games Master with his half-lidded eyes.

"Mortal man," he began, "you fear me because you do not understand me. You are a daysider with but one life in you, and when that is gone, you will have no more. We of darkness are said not to have souls, such as you are alleged to possess. We do, however, live many times, by means of a process which you cannot share. I say that you are jealous of this, that you mean to deprive me of a life. Know that dying is just as hard for one of us as it is for one of you."

The Games Master dropped his eyes.

"It is not—" he began.

"Accept my offer," Jack interrupted, "to

17

absent myself from your games. Allow your order to be fulfilled, and it will be you who will be the ultimate loser."

The hunchback stopped writing and turned toward Benoni.

"Jack," said the Games Master, "you *did* come to steal it, didn't you?"

"Of course I did."

"Why? It would be hard to dispose of. It is so distinctive—"

"It was for a friend to whom I owe a favor. He desired the bauble. Release me and I will tell him that I failed, which will be no less than the truth."

"I do not seek your wrath upon your return—"

"What you seek will mean little compared to what you will receive, if you make that trip necessary."

". . . Yet a man in my position cannot readily bring himself to trust one who is also known as Jack of Liars."

"Then my word means nothing to you?"

"I am afraid not." And to the scribe he said, "Continue your writing."

". . . And my threats mean nothing?"

"They cause me some concern. But I must weigh your vengeance—several years removed—against the immediate penalties I will suffer if the Hellflame is stolen. Try to understand my position, Jack."

"I do indeed," he said, turning toward Smage and Quazer. "You of the jackass ears and you—gynandromorph!—neither will you be forgotten!"

Smage looked at Quazer, and Quazer batted his eyelashes and smiled. "You may tell it to our patron, the Lord of Bats," he said.

Jack's face changed as his ancient enemy's name was spoken.

Because magic is slowed in Twilight, where science begins, it was perhaps half a minute before a bat entered the tent and passed between them. During this time, Quazer had said, "We compete beneath the banner of the Bat."

Jack's laughter was broken by the creature's passage. When he saw it, he lowered his head and the muscles at the hinges of his jaws tightened.

The silence that followed was interrupted only by the scratching of the quill.

Then, "So be it," said Jack.

They took Jack to the center of the compound, where the man named Blite stood with his huge axe. Jack looked away quickly, and licked his lips. Then his eyes were drawn irresistibly back to the blade's bright edge.

Before he was asked to kneel at the chopping block, the air about him came alive with leathery missiles that he knew to be a horde of dancing bats. More of them poured in from the west, but they moved too quickly to cast him shadows that mattered.

He cursed then, knowing that his enemy had sent his minions to mock him in his passing.

When it came to a theft, he generally succeeded. He was irritated at having to lose one of his lives on a sloppy job. After all, he was who he was . . .

He knelt and lowered his head.

As he waited, he wondered whether it was true that the head retained consciousness for a second or two after being severed from the body. He attempted to dismiss it, but the thought kept returning.

But could it be, he wondered, more than simply a botched job? If the Lord of Bats had laid a trap, it could only mean that one thing.

2

FINE LINES OF light traced in the blackness—white, silver, blue, yellow, red—mainly straight, but sometimes wavering. They crossed the entire field of darkness, and some were brighter than others . . .

Slowing, slowing . . .

Finally, the lines were no longer infinite roadways or strands of a web.

They were long thin rods—then sticks—hyphens of light . . .

Ultimately, they were winking points.

For a long while he regarded the stars uncomprehendingly. It was only after a great time that the word "stars" seeped into his consciousness from somewhere, and a tiny glimmer began behind his staring eyes.

Silence, and no sensations but seeing . . .

And again after a long while, he felt himself falling—falling as from a great height, gaining in substance, until he realized that he was lying on his back staring upward with the full weight of his being once again on him.

"I am Shadowjack," he said within himself, still unable to move.

He did not know where he was lying or how he had come to that place of darkness and stars. The sensation seemed familiar; however, the return felt like something previously experienced, though long ago.

A warmth about his heart spread outward, and he felt a tingling that quickened all his senses. With this he knew.

"Damn!" was the first word he spoke, for with the return of his sense of smell came a full awareness of his situation.

He was lying in the Dung Pits of Glyve at the West Pole of the World in the realm of the sinister Baron of Drekkheim, through whose kingdom all who seek resurrection must pass.

He realized therefore that he was on a mound of offal in the middle of a lake of filth. An evil smile crossed his face as he considered for the hundredth time that while men begin and end in such fashion, darksiders could claim nothing better.

When he could move his right hand, he began to rub his throat and massage his neck.

There was no pain, but that last dreadful memory came vividly to mind. How long ago had it been? Several years, most likely, he decided. That was average for him. He shuddered and forced away the momentary thought of the time when his last life would be expended. This shudder was followed by a shivering which did not cease. He cursed the loss of the garments which by now had either moldered with his former body or, more likely, had been worn to tatters on the back of another man.

He rose slowly, requiring air but wishing that he could forego breathing for a time. He tossed aside the eggshaped stone he had found in his hand. It would not do to remain long in one place now that he was almost himself again.

The East was in all directions. Gritting his teeth, he chose what he hoped to be the easiest way.

He did not know how long it took him to achieve the shore. Though his shadow eyes quickly accustomed him to the starlight, there were no true shadows for him to consult.

And what is time? A year is one complete passage of a planet about its sun. Any subdivisions of that year may be determined in accordance with other motions of the planet . . . or the motions of its inhabitants.

For Jack, the four annual fluctuations of the Twilight represented seasons. Within these time units, dates were always to be determined more specifically by means of the stars—which were always visible—and the application of magical principles to determine the moods of their governing spirits. He knew that the daysiders possessed mechanical and electrical devices for keeping track of time because he had stolen several of these. But since they had failed to function darkside, they had been of no use to him except as trinkets to pass on to tavern girls as amulets of great contraceptive power.

Stripped and stinking, Jack stood upon the shore of that dark and silent place. After catching his breath and recovering his strength, he began his eastward trek.

The land slanted slightly upward, and there were puddles and pools of filth all about him as he made his way. Rivers of it ran to the lake, since all filth eventually comes to Glyve. Fountains occasionally erupted, jetting high and spattering him as he passed. There were cracks and crevasses from which the odor of sulfur dioxide constantly arose. Hurrying, he held his nose and prayed to his tutelary deities. He doubted that his petition would be heard, however, since he did not feel that the gods would devote much attention to anything emitted from this particular portion of the world.

Moving on, he rested little. The ground continued to slope upward, and after a time small crops of rock began to appear. Shivering, he picked his way among them. He had forgotten—purposely, of course—many of the worst features of this place. Small, sharp stones tore into his soles, so he knew that he tracked bloody footprints as he went. Faintly, at his back, he could hear the sound of the many-footed things that emerged to lick at them. It was said to be bad luck to look back at this point.

It was always with a certain sadness that he reflected on the loss of blood from any new body which also happened to be his own. The texture of the ground changed as he advanced, however, and soon it was smooth rock on which he trod. Later, he noted with satisfaction that the sounds of feet had died away.

Mounting ever higher, he was pleased by the diminution of the odors. He reflected that this could simply be the result of a numbing of his olfactory abilities after the steady bombardment they had endured. This fact, whatever its cause, seemed to give his body time to consider other matters; and of course his mind followed. In addition to being filthy, sore and tired, he now realized that he was hungry and thirsty as well.

Struggling with his memory as he would with a warehouse door, he entered and sought. He retraced his previous journeys from Glyve, recalling every detail that he could. But, seeking as he walked, no correspondences came, no familiar landmarks.

When he skirted a small stand of metallic

trees, he realized that he had never come this way before.

There will be no clean water for miles, he thought, unless Fortune nods and I come upon a rainpool. But it rains so seldom in this place . . . It is a land of filth, not cleanliness. If I tried a small magic for rain, something would note it and seek me. I would be easy prey as I now stand without shadows. Then I would either live in a vile way or be slain and be returned to the Dung Pits. I'll walk till death is near, *then* try for rain.

Later, his eyes caught sight of an unnatural object in the distance. He approached it warily and saw that it was twice his height and a double armspan in width. It was of stone and its facing surface was smooth. He read there the carved, large-lettered message which in the common darkside tongue said: WELCOME SLAVE.

Beneath it was the Great Seal of Drekkheim.

Jack felt a great sense of relief, for it was known to a few—those few who had escaped the Baron's service and with whom Jack had discussed the subject—that such markers were placed in the most lightly patrolled areas of the realm. The hope was that a returnee would then undertake a lengthy detour, entering some area where the chances of capture would be better.

Jack moved past it and would have spat, but his mouth was too dry.

As he moved forward his strength continued

to leave him, and it took him longer to regain his balance each time he slipped. He knew that he had missed what ordinarily would have been several sleep-periods. Yet he saw no place that appeared safe enough for sleeping.

It grew more and more difficult for him to keep his eyes open. At one point, as he stumbled and fell, he was certain that he had just awakened from sleep-walking a great distance, unaware of the area through which he had passed. The present terrain was more rugged than that which he had last remembered noting. This gave him a glimmer of hope which, in turn, provided sufficient resolve for him to rise once more.

Shortly thereafter, he saw the place that would have to be his haven, for he could go no farther.

It was a place of tumbled, leaning stones, near to the foot of a sharp slope of rock which led on to even higher ground. He scouted the area, crawling as best he could, seeking signs of life.

Detecting nothing, he entered. He moved as far within the stony maze as he could go, found a reasonably level spot, collapsed there and slept.

He had no way of telling how much later it was when it occurred; but something within the deep pool that is sleep came to him and told him. Drowner-like, he struggled toward the distant surface.

27

He felt the kiss upon his throat and the alb of her long hair that lay on his shoulders.

For a moment he rested there, trying to muster his remaining strength. He seized her hair with his left hand, as his right arm moved about her body. Forcing her away from him, he rolled to his left, knowing from his waking instant what must be done. With just a fraction of his old speed, his head dropped forward.

When he had finished, he wiped his mouth, stood and stared down at the limp form.

"Poor vampire," he said. "There was not much blood in you which is why you wanted mine so desperately, yet were so weak in its taking. But I, too, was desperate in my hunger. We do what we must."

Wearing the black skirts, cloak and tight-fitting boots he had appropriated, Jack moved onto higher ground now, occasionally crossing fields of black grasses that wrapped about his ankles and attempted to stop him. Familiar with these, he kicked his way through before they could fasten too tightly. He had no desire to become fertilizer.

Finally, he located a rainpool. He observed it for hours, from many vantages, for it would be an ideal spot to snare a returnee. Having come to the conclusion that it was unguarded, he approached it, studied it, then fell to the ground and drank for a long while. He rested, drank again, rested again, and drank once more, regretting that he lacked the means to carry some of it away with him.

Still regretting, he stripped and washed the filth from his body.

Later, he passed flowers that had the appearance of rooted snakes—or perhaps they were indeed rooted snakes. They hissed and threw themselves flat in their attempts to reach him.

He slept twice more before he located another rainpool. This one was guarded, however, and it took all the stealth and cunning of a thief to obtain a drink. Since he also obtained the dozing guard's sword, and since the man then had no further use for it, Jack supplied himself with the bread, cheese, wine and change of clothing which were available there.

The rations were sufficient for one meal. This, in addition to the fact that there was no mount in the vicinity, led him to the conclusion that there was a guard post in the neighborhood and that relief might be arriving at any time. He drank the wine and refilled the flask with water, damning the smallness of the container.

Then, as there were no nearby crevasses or caves wherein he might secrete the remains, he departed quickly, leaving what remained there.

He ate slowly as he moved, his stomach at first protesting this strange invasion of privacy. He finished half the food in this fashion and saved the rest. Occasionally, he would see a small animal. He took to carrying several stones in his hands, with the hope of bringing one down. But they all proved too fast, or he too slow. He did, however, gain a good piece of flint when renewing his supply of stones for the seventh time.

Later, he hid himself when he heard the sound of hoofbeats, but no one passed near. He knew that he was deep into Drekkheim now, and he wondered toward which of its boundaries he was headed. He shuddered when he considered that at one point it abutted the westernmost boundary of that nameless realm which held High Dudgeon, place of power and keep of the Lord of Bats.

Toward the bright stars, from the dark ground, he hurled another petition, for whatever it was worth.

Climbing, circling, sometimes running, his hatred grew more rapidly than the hunger within him.

Smage, Quazer, Benoni, Blite the executioner and the Lord of Bats . . .

One by one he would seek them and have his revenge upon them, beginning with the lesser and building his power as he went, until the encounter with the one who even now might be too near for safe dreaming.

Nor did he dream well.

He dreamed that he was back in the Dung

Pits. This time, however, he was chained, so that like Morningstar—who sits forever at the Gates of Dawn—he must remain in that place forever.

He awakened drenched with perspiration, despite the slight chill in the air. It seemed as if the noxious odors of that place had come to him briefly and in their fullest intensity once again.

It was not until considerably later that he was able to finish his rations.

But the hatred sustained him; it nourished him. It quenched his thirst or caused him to forget it. It gave him the strength to walk another league whenever his body bade him to lie down.

He plotted their ends, again and again. He saw the racks and the pincers, the flames and the braces. He heard their screams and their pleas. In the lower chambers of his mind, he saw the gobbets of flesh and gouts of blood and rivers of tears he would extract from them before he allowed them to die.

. . . And he knew that despite the pains of this journey, it was the wound in his pride that stung most. To be taken so easily, handled so casually, dismissed so abruptly—it was like the swatting of an annoying insect. They did not treat him as if he were the power that walked the shadowland, but rather as if he were a *common* thief!

This is why he thought in terms of torture rather than a simple sword thrust. They had hurt his feelings by killing him in this manner.

Had they done it differently, he might have been less aggrieved. The Lord of Bats, it was he whose guile stirred by envy and revenge had planned such an insult. He would pay.

Hating, he drove himself onward. Although the hatred warmed him, it did not serve to prevent an increasing awareness that the temperature was growing colder. This was so despite the fact that he had not attained a significantly greater altitude for a long while.

He lay upon his back and studied the dark globe that occluded stars at midheaven. It was the focus of the Shield forces—that sphere held perpetually away from dayside's light—and someone should be seeing to its maintenance. Where were the seven Powers of the listing in the Book of Ells, whose turn it would be to run Shield duty? Surely, whatever the internecine warfare of the moment, no Power would fail to observe a Shield truce when the fate of the entire world depended on it. Jack himself had run it countless times—even in league with the Lord of Bats on two occasions.

He longed to essay the spell which would give him sight of the current page of the Book of Ells, to see whose names were recorded there. It occurred to him that one of them might be his own. But he had not heard his name spoken since his awakening in the Dung Pits. No, it must be another, he decided.

Opening his being, he could feel the terrible

cold of the outer darkness as it seeped about the edges of the orb at the Shield's apex. It was only an initial leakage, but the longer they waited the more difficult the sealing would be. It was too important to take chances with. The spell-wrought Shield kept the darkside from freezing into Allwinter as surely as their force screens prevented the daysiders from frying in the merciless glare of the sun. Jack closed his being to the inner chill.

Later, he succeeded in slaying a small, dark-furred creature as it dozed atop a rock. He skinned it and cleaned it with his blade, and as he had not come across any kindling he ate the meat raw. He cracked its bones with his teeth and sucked the marrow from them. He detested such rude living, although there were those among his acquaintances who preferred it to the more civilized. He was pleased that there were none to witness his repast.

As he walked on, there came a tingling within his ears.

Jack of Shadows, and . . .

That was all.

Whoever had spoken had had a shadow fall across his lips at that moment. It had been all too brief, however.

Jack turned his head slowly and knew the direction. It had been far ahead and to his right. Over a hundred leagues, he guessed. Possibly even in another kingdom.

He gnashed his teeth. If only he knew his present location, he could at least guess as to the source. As it was, he could have heard anything from a fragment of a tavern tale to a piece of a plot by someone already aware of his return. The possibility of the latter occupied his mind for a long while.

He increased his pace and did not rest at the time he had planned. He decided that this hastened his good fortune, when he discovered a rainpool. He found it free of surveillance, approached it and drank his fill.

He could not quite make out his reflection in the dark waters, so he strained his eyes until his features became faintly discernible: dark face, thin, faint lights for eyes, silhouette of a man with stars at his back.

"Ah, Jack! You've become a shadow yourself!" he muttered. "Wasting away in a cruel land. All because you promised the Colonel Who Never Died that cursed bauble! Never thought it would come to this, did you? Was the attempt worth the price of failure?" Then he laughed, for the first time since his resurrection. "Are you laughing, too, shadow of a shadow?" he finally asked his reflection. "Probably," he decided. "But you are being polite about it because you are *my* reflection, and you know I'll go after the bloody jewel again, as soon as I know where it lies. She's worth it."

For a moment he forgot his hatred and

smiled. The flames that burned at the back of his mind died down and were replaced by the image of the girl.

She had a pale face, with eyes the green of the edges of old mirrors. Her short upper lip touched the lower moistly in a faint pout. Her chin fit within the circle of his thumb and forefinger, and copper, catenary bangs flowed over matching brows like the wings of a hovering bird. Evene was her name and she stood up to his shoulder in height. She wore green velvet to a narrow waist. Her neck was like the bark-stripped base of a lovely tree. Her fingers moved like dancers on the strings of the *palmyrin*. This was Evene of the Fortress Holding.

Born of one of those rare unions between darkness and light, the Colonel Who Never Died was her father and a mortal woman named Loret her mother. Could that be a part of the fascination? he wondered once more. Since she's part of light, does she possess a soul? That must be it, he decided. He could not picture her as a darkside power, moving as he moved, emerging from the Dung Pits of Glyve. No! He banished the thought immediately.

The Hellflame was the bride-price her father had set, and he vowed to go after it again. First, of course, came the vengeance . . . But Evene would understand. She knew of his honor, his pride. She would wait. She had said that she would wait forever, that day he had departed

35

for Iglés and the Hellgames there. Being her father's daughter, time would mean little to her. She would outlive mortal women in youth, beauty and grace. She would wait.

"Yes, shadow of a shadow," he said to his other self within the pool. "She's worth it."

Hurrying through the darkness, wishing his feet were wheels, Jack heard the sound of hooves once more. Again he hid himself, and again they passed. Only this time they passed much nearer.

He did not hear his name spoken again, but he wondered whether there was any connection between the words he had heard and the riders who had come near.

The temperature did not decrease, not did it rise again. A constant chill was with him always, and whenever he opened his being he could feel the slow, steady leakage in the Shield above him. It would be most noticeable in this land, he reasoned, since the Dung Pits of Glyve lay directly beneath the Shield's apex, the sphere. Perhaps the effects had not yet been felt farther east.

He travelled on and he slept, and there were no further sounds which could be taken as pursuit. Heartened, he rested more frequently and occasionally deviated from the route he had set by the stars to investigate formations which might hold rainpools or animal life. On two such occasions he located water, but he found nothing that would provide nourishment.

On one such excursion he was attracted by a pale red glow coming through a cleft in the rock to his right. Had he been moving more quickly, he would have passed it unnoticed, so feeble was the light that emerged. As it was, he was picking his way up a slope, over gravel and loose stones.

When he saw it, he paused and wondered. Fire? If something was burning, there would be shadows. And if there were shadows . . .

He drew his blade and turned sidewise. Sword arm first, he entered the cleft. He eased himself along the narrow passage, resting his back against the stone between steps.

Looking upward, he estimated the top of the rocky mass at four times his own height. A river of stars flowed through the greater blackness of the stone.

The passage gradually turned to the left, then terminated abruptly, opening onto a wide ledge that stood perhaps three feet above the valley's floor. He stood there and considered the place.

It was closed on all sides by high and seemingly natural walls of stone. Black shrubbery grew along the bases of these walls, and dark weeds and grasses grew at a greater distance from them. All vegetation ceased, however, at the perimeter of a circle.

It lay at the far end of the valley, and its diameter was perhaps eighty feet. It was perfectly circumscribed and there were no signs of life within it. A huge mossy boulder stood at its center, glowing faintly.

Jack felt uneasy, though he could not say why. He surveyed the pinnacles and escarpments that hedged the valley. He glanced at the stars.

Was it his imagination, or did the light flicker once while his eyes were elsewhere?

He stepped down from the ledge. Then, cautiously, keeping close to the lefthand wall, he advanced.

The moss covered the boulder entirely. It was pinkish in color, and it seemed to be the source of the glow. As he neared it, Jack noted that it was not nearly as cold in the valley as it was outside it. Perhaps the walls provided some insulation.

Blade in hand, Jack entered the circle and advanced. Whatever the cause of the strangeness of this place, he reasoned that it might be a thing he could turn to his advantage.

But he had taken scarcely half a dozen steps within the circle, when he felt a psychic stirring like something bumping, nuzzling against his mind.

Fresh marrow! I cannot be contained! came the thought.

Jack halted.

"Who are you? Where are you?" he asked.

I lie before you, little one. Come to me.

"I see just a moldy rock."

Soon you will see more. Come to me!

"No thank you," said Jack, feeling a growing sinister intent behind the aroused consciousness which had addressed him.

It is not an invitation. It is a command that I place upon you.

He felt a strong force come into him, and with it a compulsion to move forward. He resisted mightily and asked, "What are you?"

I am that which you see before you. Come now!

"The rock or the fungus?" he inquired, struggling to remain where he stood and feeling that he was losing the contest. Once he took one step, he knew the second would come more easily. His will would be broken and the rock thing would have its way with him.

Say that I am both, although we are really one.— You are stubborn, creature. This is good. Now, however, you can no longer resist me.

It was true, His right leg was attempting to move of its own accord, and he realized that in a moment it would. So he compromised.

Turning his body, he yielded to the pressure, but the step that he took was more to the right than straight ahead.

Then his left foot began inching its way in the direction of the rock. Struggling while submitting, he moved to the side as well as ahead.

Very well. Though you will not come to me in a straight line, yet will you come to me.

The perspiration appeared on Jack's brow

as step by step he fought; and step by step he advanced in a counterclockwise spiral toward that which summoned him. He was uncertain as to how long it was that he struggled. He forgot everything: his hatred, his hunger, his thirst, his love. There were only two things in the universe, himself and the pink boulder. The tension between them filled the air like a steady note which goes unheard after a time because of its constancy, which makes it a normal part of things. It was as if the struggle between Jack and the other had been going on forever.

Then something else entered the tight little universe of their conflict.

Forty or fifty painful steps—he had lost count—brought Jack into a position where he could see the far side of the boulder. It was then that his concentration almost gave way to a quick blazing of emotion and nearly allowed him to succumb to the tugging of that other will.

He staggered as he beheld the heap of skeletons that were lying behind the glowing stone.

Yes. I must position them there so that newcomers to this place will not grow fearful and avoid the circle of my influence. It is there that you, too, will lie, bloody one.

Recovering his self-control, Jack continued the duel, the piles of bones adding tangible incentive to the effort. He passed behind the boulder in his slow, circling motion, passed the bones and continued on. Soon he stood before it as he had done earlier, only now he was about ten feet nearer. The spiral continued and he found himself approaching the back side once again.

I must say that you are taking longer than any of the others. But then you are the first who thought to circle as you resigned yourself to me.

Jack did not reply, but as he rounded to the rear he studied the grisly remains. During his passage, he noted that swords and daggers, metal buckles and harness straps lay there intact; garments and other items of fabric appeared, for the most part, half-rotted. The spillage from several knapsacks lay upon the ground, but he could not positively identify all the small items by starlight. Still, if indeed he had seen what he thought he saw lying there among the bones, then a meager measure of hope, he decided, was allowable.

Once more around and you will come to me, little thing. You will touch me then.

As he moved, Jack drew nearer and nearer to the mottled, pink surface of the thing. It seemed to grow larger with each step, and the pale light it shed became more and more diffuse. No single point that he regarded seemed to possess luminescence of its own; the glow seemed an effect of the total surface.

Back to the front and within spitting distance . . .

Moving around to the side now, so close that he could almost reach out and touch it . . .

He transferred his blade to his left hand and struck out with it, gashing the mossy surface. A liquid appeared in the mark he had made.

You cannot hurt me that way. You cannot hurt me at all.

The skeletons came into view again, and he was very close to that surface which looked like cancerous flesh. He could feel it hungering for him, and he was kicking bones aside and hearing them crunch beneath his boots as he moved to the rear. He saw what he wanted and forced himself to go another three steps to reach it, though it was like walking against a hurricane. He was just inches from that deadly surface now.

He threw himself toward the knapsacks. He raked them toward him—using both his blade and his hand—and he snatched also at the rotted cloaks and jackets that lay about him.

Then came an irresistible pull, and he felt himself moving backward until his shoulder touched the lichen-covered stone.

He tried to drag himself away, knowing in advance that he would fail.

For a moment he felt nothing. Then an icy sensation began at the point of contact. This quickly faded and was gone. There was no pain. He realized then that the shoulder had grown completely numb.

It is not as terrible as you feared, is it?

Then, like a man who has been sitting for hours and rises too quickly, a wave of dark dizziness rushed through his head. This passed, but when it did he became aware of a new sensation. It was as though a plug had been pulled in his shoulder. He felt his strength draining away. With each heartbeat it became more difficult to think clearly. The numbness began to spread across his back and down his arm. It was difficult to raise his right hand and grope for the bag at his belt. He fumbled with it for what seemed to be ages.

Resisting a strong impulse to close his eyes and lower his head to his chest, he heaped the rags he had gathered into a mound before him. With his left hand aching upon its hilt, he moved his blade beside the pile and struck it with the flint. The sparks danced upon the dry cloth, and he continued to strike them even after the smoldering had begun.

When the first flame arose, he used it to light the candle stub some dead man had carried.

He held it before him and there were shadows.

He set it upon the ground, and he knew that his shadow lay upon the boulder now.

What are you doing, dinner?

Jack rested in his gray realm, his head clear once more, the old, familiar tingle beginning in his fingertips and toes.

43

I am the stone who gets blood from men! Answer me! What are you doing?

The candle flickered, the shadows caressed him. He placed his right hand upon his left shoulder and the tingling entered there and the numbness departed. Then, wrapping himself in shadows, he rose to his feet.

"Doing?" he said. "No. Done. You have been my guest. Now I feel it only fair that you reciprocate."

He moved away from the boulder and turned to face it. It reached out for him as it had before, but this time he moved his arms and the shadows played upon its surface. He extended his being into the twisting kaleidoscopic pattern he had created.

Where are you?

"Everywhere," he said. "Nowhere."

Then he sheathed his blade and returned to the boulder. As the candle was but a stub, he knew that he must act quickly. He placed the palms of his hands upon the spongy surface.

"Here I am," he said.

Unlike the other darkside Lords, whose places of power were fixed geographical localities where they reigned supreme, Jack's was more a tenuous one, and liable to speedy cancellation, but it existed wherever light and objects met to make a lesser darkness.

With the lesser darkness about him, Jack placed his will upon the boulder.

There was, of course, resistance as he reversed their previous roles. The power that had compelled him fought back, became the victim itself. Within himself, Jack stimulated the hunger, the open space, the vacuum. The current, the drain, the pull was reversed.

. . . And he fed.

You may not do this to me. You are a thing.

But Jack laughed and grew stronger as its resistance ebbed. Soon it was unable even to protest.

Before the candle bloomed brightly and died, the mosses had turned brown and the glow had departed. Whatever had once lived there lived no longer.

Jack wiped his hands on his cloak, many times, before he departed the valley.

3

THE STRENGTH HE had gathered sustained him for a long while, and Jack hoped that soon he might quit the stinking realm. The temperature did not diminish further, and there came one light rainfall as he was preparing to sleep. He huddled beside a rock and drew his cloak over his head. It did not protect him completely, but he laughed even as the waters reached his skin. It was the first rainfall he had felt since Glyve.

Later, there were sufficient pools and puddles for him to clean himself as well as to drink and to refill his flask. He continued on rather than sleep, so his garments might dry more quickly.

It brushed past his face so rapidly that he barely had time to react. It happened as he neared a shattered tower that a piece of the darkness broke away and dropped toward him, moving in a rapid, winding way.

He did not have sufficient time to draw his blade. It passed his face and darted away. He managed to hurl all three stones which he carried before it was out of sight, coming close to hitting it with the second one. Then he bowed his head and cursed for a full half-minute. It had been a bat.

Wishing for shadows, he began to run.

There were many broken towers upon the plain, and one at the mouth of a pass led between high hills and into the range of mountains they faced. Because Jack did not like passing near structures—ruined or otherwise—which might house enemies, he attempted to skirt it at as great a distance as possible.

He had passed it and was drawing near the cleft when he heard his name called out.

"Jack! My Shadowjack!" came the cry. "It's you! It really is!"

He spun to face the direction from which the words had come, his hand on the hilt of his blade.

"Nay! Nay, my Jackie! You need no swords with old Rosie!"

He almost missed her, so motionless did she stand: a crone, dressed in black, leaning upon a staff, a broken wall at her back.

"How is it that you know my name?" he finally asked.

"Have you forgotten me, darlin' Jack? Forgotten me? Say you haven't . . ."

He studied the bent form with its nest of white and gray hair.

A broken mop, he thought. She reminds me of a broken mop.

Yet . . .

There was something familiar about her. He could not say what.

He let his hand drop from the weapon. He moved toward her.

"Rosie?"

No. I could not be . . .

He drew very near. Finally, he was staring down, looking into her eyes.

"Say you remember, Jack."

"I remember," he said.

And he did.

". . . Rosalie, at the Sign of the Burning Pestle, on the coach road near the ocean. But that was so long ago, and in Twilight . . ."

"Yes," she said. "It was so long ago and so far away. But I never forgot you, Jack. Of all the men that tavern girl met, she remembered you the best. —What has become of you, Jack?"

"Ah, my Rosalie! I was beheaded—wrongfully, I hasten to add—and I am just now returning from Glyve.—But what of you? You're not a darksider. You're mortal. What are you doing in the horrid realm of Drekkheim?"

"I am the Wise Woman of the Eastern Marches, Jack. I'll admit I was not very wise in my youth—to be taken in by your ready smile and your promises—but I learned better as I grew older. I nursed an old bawd in her failing years and she taught me something of the Art. When I learned the Baron had need of a Wise Woman to guard this passage to his kingdom, I came and swore allegiance to him. 'Tis said he is a wicked man, but he has always been good to old Rosie. Better than most she's known.—It is good that you remembered me."

Then she produced a cloth parcel from beneath her cloak, unfastened it and spread it open upon the ground.

"Sit and break bread with me, Jack," she said. "It will be like old times."

He removed his sword belt and seated himself across the cloth from her.

"It's been a long while since you ate the living stone," she said; and she passed him bread and a piece of dried meat. "So I know that you are hungry."

"How is it that you know of my encounter with the stone?"

"I am, as I said, a Wise Woman—in the technical sense of the term. I did not know it was your doing, but I knew that the stone had been destroyed. This is the reason I patrol this place for the Baron. I keep aware of all that occurs and of all who pass this way. I report these things to him."

"Oh," said Jack.

"There must have been something to all your boasting—that you were not a mere dark-sider, but a Lord, a Power, albeit a poor one," she said. "For all my figuring has told me that only one such could have eaten the red rock. You were not just jesting then when you boasted to that poor girl about that thing. Other things, perhaps, but not that thing . . ."

"What other things?" he asked.

"Things such as saying you would come back for her one day and take her to dwell with you in Shadow Guard, that castle no man has ever set eyes upon. You told her that, and she waited many years. Then one night an old bawd took ill at the inn. The young girl—who was no longer a young girl—had her future to think about. She made a bargain to learn a better trade."

Jack was silent for a time, staring at the ground. He swallowed the bread he had been chewing, then, "I went back," he said. "I went back, and no one even remembered my Rosalie. Everything was changed. All the people were different. I went away again."

She cackled.

"Jack! Jack! Jack!" she said. "There's no need for your pretty lies now. It makes no difference to an old woman the things a young girl believed."

"You say you are a Wise Woman," he said. "Have you no better way than guessing to tell the truth from a lie?"

"I'd not use the Art against a Power—" she began.

"Use it," he said; and he looked into her eyes once more.

She squinted and leaned forward, her gaze boring into his own. Her eyes were suddenly vast caverns opened to engulf him. He bore the falling sensation that came with this. It vanished seconds later when she looked away from him, turning her head to rest upon her right shoulder.

"You *did* go back," she said.

"It was as I told you."

He picked up his bread and began to chew noisily, so as not to appear to notice the moisture which had appeared upon her cheek.

"I forgot," she finally said. "I forgot how little time means to a darksider. The years mean so little to you that you do not keep proper track of them. You simply decided one day that you would go back for Rosie, never thinking that she might have become an old woman and died or gone away. I understand now, Jackie. You are used to things that never change. The Powers remain the Powers. You may kill a man today and have dinner with him ten years hence, laughing over the duel you fought and trying to recall its cause. Oh, it's a good life you lead!"

"I do not have a soul. You do."

"A soul?" she laughed. "What's a soul? I've never seen one. How do I know it's there? Even so, what good has it done me? I'd trade it in a twinkling to be like one of you. It's beyond my Art, though."

"I'm sorry," Jack said.

They ate in silence for a time. "There is a thing I would like to ask you," she said.

"What is that?"

"Is there really a Shadow Guard?" she asked him. "A castle of high, shadow-decked halls, invisible to your enemies and friends alike, where you would have taken that girl to spend her day with you?"

"Of course," he told her; and he watched her eat. She was missing many teeth and had a tendency to smack her lips now. But suddenly, behind her net of wrinkles, he saw the face of the young girl she had been. White teeth had flashed when she had smiled, and her hair had been long and glossy, as the darkside sky between stars. And there had been a certain luster in eyes the blue of dayside skies he had looked upon. He had liked to think it was only there for him.

She must not have much longer to live, he thought. As the girl's face vanished, he regarded the sagging flesh beneath her chin.

"Of course," he repeated, "and now that

I've found you, will you accompany me back? Out of this wretched land and into a place of comforting shadows? Come spend the rest of your days with me, and I will be kind to you."

She studied his face.

"You would keep your promise after all these years—now that I'm an ugly old lady?"

"Let us go through the pass and journey back toward Twilight together."

"Why would you do this for me?"

"You know why."

"Quickly, give me your hands!" she said.

He extended his hands and she seized them, turning both palms upward. She leaned far forward and scrutinized them.

"Ah! It is no use!" she said. "I cannot read you, Jack. The hands of a thief make too many twists and turns and manipulations. The lines are all wrong—though they are magnificently ruined hands!"

"What is it that you see but do not wish to tell me, Rosalie?"

"Do not finish eating. Take your bread and run. I am too old to go with you. It was sweet of you to ask. That young girl might have liked Shadow Guard, but I am content to spend my days where I am.—Go now. Hurry! And try to forgive me."

"Forgive you for what?"

She raised and kissed each of his hands.

"When I saw the approach of him whom I

had hated all these years, I sent a message by means of my Art and resolved to detain you here. Now I know that I did wrong. But the Baron's guard must already be hurrying in this direction. Enter the pass and stop for nothing. You may be able to elude them on the other side. I will try to raise a storm to obscure your trail."

He sprang to his feet, drew her to hers.

"Thank you," he said. "But what did you see in my palm?"

"Nothing."

"Tell me, Rosalie."

"It does not matter so much if they capture you," she said, "for there is a Power greater than the Baron that you would face, and face him you will. What happens then is crucial. Do not let your hatred lead you to the machine that thinks like a man, only faster. There is too much power involved, and such power and hatred would not go well together."

"Such machines only exist dayside."

"I know. Go now, Jackie boy. Go!"

He kissed her forehead.

"I will see you again one day," he said, and turning, he dashed toward the pass.

As she watched him go she was suddenly aware of the chill that had descended upon the land.

Beginning low and rising steadily, the foothills soon towered above him. He ran on, seeing them give way to high, slanting walls of stone. The pass widened, narrowed, and widened again. Finally, he pushed his panic away, held it at arms' length and slowed to a walk. It would serve no purpose to tire himself quickly; a steady, slower pace would allow him to cover more ground before fatigue overtook him.

He breathed deeply and listened for the sounds of pursuit. He heard nothing.

A long, black snake flowed along the wall at his right, vanished into a cleft in the rock, and did not reappear. Above him, a shooting star burnt its sudden way through the sky. Veins of minerals glittered like glass in the starlight.

He thought of Rosalie and wondered what it would have been like to have had parents, to have been a child, to have depended on others to assure his welfare. He wondered what it was like to be old and know that you were going to die and not return again. He grew tired of these thoughts after a time just as he had grown tired of everything. He felt a strong desire to lie down, wrap his cloak about him and sleep.

He did things to keep awake. He counted his paces—a thousand, then a thousand more; he rubbed his eyes; he hummed several songs all the way through; he reviewed spells and incantations; he thought of food; he thought of women; he thought of his greatest thefts; he counted a thousand more paces; he rehearsed tortures and ignominies; and finally he thought of Evene.

The high walls soon began to descend.

He moved among foothills, similar to those where he had entered. There were still no sounds of pursuit—indicating, he hoped, that he would not be caught in the pass. Once he struck open country again there would be more places where he could hide himself.

There came a rumble from overhead, and he looked up to see that the stars were partly obscured by clouds. They had gathered quickly, he realized; and he remembered Rosalie's promise to try to raise a storm to obscure his trail. He smiled as the lightning flashed, the thunder boomed and the first small drops began to strike about him.

When he emerged from the pass, he was drenched once more. The storm showed no sign of abating. The visibility was poor, but it appeared that he had entered upon a rock-strewn plain similar to the one he had left on the other side of the mountains.

He deviated over a mile from what he felt to be his course; that is, the most expedient route of departure from the Baron's realm. Then he sought and found a group of boulders. He encamped on the driest side of the largest and slept.

He was awakened by the sound of hoofbeats. He lay there listening and determined that it came from the direction of the pass. He drew his blade and held it at his side. The rain still fell, but lightly now; the occasional peal of thunder that he heard came from a great distance.

The hoofbeats grew fainter. He pressed his ear to the ground, sighed, and then smiled. He was still safe.

Despite the protest of his aching muscles, he rose to his feet and continued on his way. He resolved to travel for as long as the rain continued to obscure as much of his trail as possible.

His boots sucked holes in the dark mud, and his clothing stuck to his body. He sneezed several times and began to tremble from the cold. Noticing a strange ache in his right hand, he looked down to see that he was still gripping his blade. He dried the weapon on the underside of his cloak and replaced it in the sheath. Through breaks in the cloud-cover, he made out familiar constellations. By these he adjusted his course eastward.

Eventually, the rain ceased. There was nothing but mud all about him. However, he continued to walk. His clothing began to dry, and the exercise expelled something of the chill he had taken.

The hoofbeats came and went again, somewhere behind him. Why spend so much effort to hunt down one person? he wondered. It had not been this way the last time that he had returned. Of course, he had never come this way before.

Either I have achieved some special significance during my deathbound time, he decided, or the Baron's men hunt those who return for the sheer sport of it. In either instance, it is best to stay clear of them. What could Rosalie have meant when she said that it does not matter so much if they capture me? It is very strange, if she saw the truth.

Later he reached higher, rockier terrain, leaving the mud below and behind. He began looking for a place to rest. The area was level, however, and he continued rather than be caught in the open.

As he struggled along, he saw what appeared to be a distant hedge of stones. Drawing nearer, he noted that they were of a lighter color than the others in the vicinity and that they appeared to be regularly spaced. They did not appear to have been shaped by the forces of nature but hand-hewn by some monomaniac whose problem involved pentagons.

He found himself a resting place on the dry side of the nearest of these, and there he slept.

He dreamed of rain and thunder once again. The thunder throbbed continuously, and the entire universe shook with its rumble. Then, for a long while, he dwelled half-aware in the borderland between sleep and wakefulness. On one side or the other, he felt that something was amiss, although he was not certain what or why this was.

I'm not wet! he decided, feeling surprise and annoyance.

Then he followed the thunder back to his body; his head was pillowed by an outflung arm. For a moment he lay there, fully awake; then he leaped to his feet, realizing they had found his trail.

The riders came into view. He counted seven.

His blade came into his hand, and he threw his cloak back over his shoulders. He ran fingers through his hair, rubbed his eyes and waited.

Over his left shoulder, high in the middle of the air, a star appeared to brighten.

He decided that it was senseless to flee on foot from mounted men, especially when he knew of no haven which he might seek. They would only run him to the ground if he fled, and by then he would be too tired to give a good battle and send at least a few of them to the Pits.

So he waited, only slightly distracted by the growing blaze in the heavens.

The cloven hooves of the seven black riders struck sparks from the stones. Their eyes, high above the ground, were like a handful of glowing embers hurled in his direction. Wisps of smoke emerged from their nostrils, and occasionally they emitted high-pitched whistling sounds. A silent, wolf-like creature ran with them, head near the ground, tail streaming. It changed direction at every point where Jack had turned while approaching the stone.

"You will be the first," he said, raising the blade.

As if it had heard his words, it raised its muzzle, howled and raced on ahead of the riders.

Jack retreated four paces and braced his back against the stone as it came toward him. He raised the blade high, as if to slash, and seized the hilt with both hands.

Its mouth was open, tongue lolled to the side, exhibiting enormous teeth in the midst of a near-human grin.

When it sprang, he brought the blade down in a semicircle and held it before him, bracing his elbows against the stone.

It did not growl, bark or howl; it screamed as it impaled itself upon the weapon.

The impact forced the air from Jack's lungs and bloodied his elbows where they rested. For a moment, his head swam, but the screaming and the rank odor of the creature kept him conscious.

After a moment, it stopped. It snapped twice at the blade, quivered and died.

He placed his foot upon the carcass and with a great, heaving twist withdrew the blade. Then he raised it once more and faced the oncoming riders.

They slowed, drew rein, and halted, perhaps a dozen paces from where he stood.

The leader—a short, hairless man of tremendous girth—dismounted and moved forward. He shook his head as he stared down at the bleeding creature.

"You should not have slain Shunder," he said. His voice was gruff and raspy. "He sought to disarm you, not to harm you."

Jack laughed.

The man looked up, his eyes flashing yellow with power behind them.

"You mock me, thief!" he said.

Jack nodded.

"If you take me alive, I will doubtless suffer at your hands," he said. "I see no reason to conceal my feelings, Baron. I mock you because I hate you. Have you nothing better to do than harass returnees?"

Stepping backward, the Baron raised his hand. At this signal, the other riders dismounted. Grinning, he drew his blade and leaned upon it.

He said, "You were trespassing in my realm, you know."

"It is the only route back from Glyve," said Jack. "All who return must cross some of your territory."

"That is true," said the Baron, "and those whom I apprehend must pay the toll: a few years in my service."

The riders flanked Jack, forming a semicircle like a half-crown of steel as they enclosed him.

"Put up your blade, shadow man," said the Baron. "If we must disarm you, you will doubtless be injured in the scuffle. I should prefer an unmaimed servant."

As the Baron spoke, Jack spat. Two of the men glanced upward and continued to stare at the sky. Suspecting an attempt to distract him, Jack did not follow their eyes.

But then another man turned his head; and seeing this, the Baron himself looked upward.

High, and at the periphery of his vision, Jack became aware of the great glow that had appeared. He turned his head then, and he saw the great sphere that raced in their direction, growing and brightening as it approached.

Quickly, he dropped his eyes. Whatever the nature of the thing, it was senseless not to take advantage of the opportunity it had provided.

He leaped forward and beheaded the gaping man who stood at the end of the arc to his right.

He was able to split the next man's skull, despite a hasty parry which came too slow as the man turned. By then, the Baron and his four retainers had turned and were upon him.

Jack parried and retreated as rapidly as he could, not venturing a riposte. He attempted to circle the stone to his left, while keeping them at bay. They moved too quickly, however, and he found himself parenthesized. Each close-range blow that he parried now caused his palm to sting and sent a tingling sensation up his arm. The blade felt heavier with each stroke.

They began to pierce his guard, little nicks and slashes appearing on his shoulder, his biceps and his thighs. Memories of the Dung Pits flashed through his mind. From the ferocity of the assault, he judged that they no longer wished to take him prisoner but to obtain vengeance for their fallen fellows.

Realizing that he would soon be hacked to pieces, Jack resolved to take the Baron with him to Glyve if at all possible. He made ready to hurl himself upon him, heedless of the others' blades, as soon as an opening appeared in the Baron's defense. It would have to come soon, he realized, for he felt himself weakening from moment to bloody moment.

As if sensing this, the Baron fought carefully, protecting himself at all times, allowing his men to lead the assault. Gasping, Jack decided he could wait no longer.

Then everything ended. Their weapons became too hot to hold as blue flames danced along the blades. As they released them and cried out, they were blinded by a flash of white light which occurred just a brief distance above their heads. Showers of sparks fell about them and the odors of combustion reached their nostrils.

"Baron," came a sugar-filled voice, "you are trespassing as well as attempting to slay my prisoner. What have you to say for yourself?"

Fear took root in his bowels and blossomed within his stomach as Jack recognized the voice.

4

SPOTS DANCING BEFORE his eyes, Jack sought shadows.

The light faded as quickly as it had come, however, and the darkness that followed seemed almost absolute. He attempted to take advantage of this Baron and his men until he touched the rock. He began to edge his way about it.

"*Your* prisoner?" he heard the Baron shout. "He is mine!"

"We have been good neighbors for a long while, Baron—since the last geography lesson I gave you," said the now discernible figure which stood atop the rock. "Perhaps a refresher course is now in order. These markers serve to indicate the boundary between our realms. The prisoner stands on my side of the marker—as do you and your men, I might add. You are, of course, a respected visitor; and the prisoner, of course, is mine."

"Lord," said the Baron, "this has always been a disputed border—and you must bear in mind, too, that I have been pursuing this man across my own realm. It seems hardly fair for you to interfere at this point."

"Fair?" came the laughing response. "Speak not to me of fairness, neighbor—nor call the prisoner a man. We both know that the boundaries are limits of power, not of law or of treaty. For as far as my power reaches from its seat, High Dudgeon, the land is mine. The same applies to you in your place. If you wish to renegotiate the boundary by a contest of forces, let us be about it now. As for the prisoner, you are aware that he is himself a Power—one of the few mobile ones. He draws his strength from no single locale, but from a condition of light and darkness. His captor cannot but benefit from his services; therefore, he is mine. Do you agree, Lord of Offal? Or shall we reestablish the boundary this moment?"

"I see that your power is with you—"

"Then we are obviously within my realm. Go home now, Baron."

Having circled to the far side of the marker, Jack made his way quietly into the darkness beyond. He had had the opportunity to spring back across the boundary and perhaps precipitate a struggle; but whatever its outcome, he would have been someone's captive. Better to fly, in the only direction open. He moved more quickly.

Glancing back, he saw what appeared to be a continuation of the argument, for the Baron was stamping about and gesturing wildly. He could hear his angry shouts, though he had come too far to distinguish the words being shouted. He broke into a run, knowing that his absence would not remain unnoticed much longer. He topped a small rise, raced down its eastern slope, cursing the loss of his blade.

He tired quickly but forced himself to move at a dog-trot, stopping only to arm himself with two easily held stones.

Then for a moment his shadow lay long before him, and he stopped and turned in his tracks. A great blaze of light had occurred beyond the hill and within it, like ashes or blown leaves, hordes of bats were eddying, rising, darting. Before he could take advantage of shadows, the light dimmed and darkness came again. The only sound now was his own heavy breathing. He glanced at the stars for guidance and hurried on, looking as he went for a hiding place from the pursuit that he knew would follow.

He kept glancing back but there was no recurrence of the phenomenon. He wondered as to the outcome of the conflict. The Baron, despite his brutish mien, was commonly known to be an uncommonly able sorcerer; also, the situation of the border indicated that both stood at the same relative distances from their places of power.

It would be pleasant, he decided, if they would annihilate one another. Although that was unlikely. Pity.

Knowing that by now his absence must have been noted and realizing that the only thing which could stay pursuit would be a drawn-out struggle, he prayed that it would be a lengthy affair, adding the observation that the ideal outcome would entail death or severe injury for all parties involved.

As if to mock his petition, it was only a brief while later that a dark form flitted past him. He hurled both his stones, but they went wide of the mark.

Resolving not to travel in a straight line, he turned to his left and headed in that direction. He was walking slowly to conserve his strength; and as perspiration evaporated, he felt the chill once again. Or was it just that?

It seemed as if a dark form paced him, far to his left. Whenever he turned his head in that direction, it vanished. Staring straight ahead, however, he detected something of a movement from the corner of his eye. It seemed to be drawing nearer.

Soon it was at his side. He felt the presence, though he could barely discern it. While it made no hostile movements, he prepared to defend himself at its first touch.

"May I inquire as to the state of your health?" came the soft, sweet voice.

Suppressing a shudder, Jack said, "I am hungry, thirsty and tired."

"How unfortunate. I will see that those conditions are soon remedied."

"Why?"

"It is my custom to treat my guests with every courtesy."

"I was not aware of my being anyone's guest."

"All visitors to my realm are my guests, Jack, even those who abused my hospitality on previous occasions."

"That is good to know—especially if it means that you will offer me assistance in reaching your eastern frontier as quickly and safely as possible."

"We will discuss the matter after dinner."

"Very good."

"This way, please."

Jack followed him as he bore to the right, knowing that it would be futile to do otherwise. As they moved, he occasionally caught a glimpse of that dark, handsome face, half-touched by starlight, half-hidden by the high, curved collar of the cloak he wore; the eyes within it were like the pools that form about the wicks of black candles: hot, dark and liquid. Bats kept dropping from out of the sky and vanishing within his cloak. After a long, silent while, he gestured toward a prominence that lay ahead.

"There," he said.

Jack nodded and studied the decapitated hill. A minor place of power, he decided, and within this one's reach.

They approached it as they climbed slowly. When Jack slipped at one point, he felt a hand upon his elbow, steadying him. He noted that the other's boots made no sound, though they passed over some gravel.

Finally, "What became of the Baron?" he inquired.

"He has gone home a wiser man," said the other; and there was a flash of white within a momentary smile.

They reached the hill's level top and moved to its center.

The dark one drew his blade and used it to scratch an elaborate pattern upon the ground. Jack recognized some of the markings. Then he motioned Jack away, moved his left thumb along the edge of the blade and let his blood fall into the center of the pattern. As he did this, he spoke seven words. He turned then and gestured for Jack to come and stand beside him once again. He then drew a circle about them and turned to address the pattern once again.

As the words were spoken, the pattern took fire at their feet. Jack sought to look away from the blazing lines and curves, but his gaze was trapped within the diagram and his eyes began to trace it.

A feeling of lethargy overcame him as the pattern took hold of his mind to the exclusion of all else. He seemed to be moving within it, a part of it . . .

Someone pushed him and he fell.

He was on his knees in a place of brilliance, and the multitudes mocked him. No.

Those who mimicked his every movement were other versions of himself.

He shook his head to clear it, realized then that he was surrounded by mirrors and brightness.

He stood, regarding the confused prospect. He was near to the center of a large, many-sided chamber. All of the walls were mirrors as were the countless facets of the concave ceiling and the gleaming floor beneath him. He was not certain as to the source of the light. Perhaps it had its origin, somehow, in the mirrors themselves. Part way up the wall to his right, a table was laid. As he approached it, he realized that he was walking up an incline, though he felt no extra strain upon his muscles nor any disturbance of his sense of equilibrium. Hurrying then, he passed the table and continued on in what he deemed to be a straight line. The table was behind him, then above him. After several hundred paces, it was before him once again.

He turned in a right angle from his course and repeated the walk. The results were the same.

There were no windows, no doors. There was the table, there was a bed and there were chairs with side-tables scattered about the various surfaces of the chamber. It was as if he were confined within an immense, luster-hoarding jewel. Reflected and re-reflected versions of himself paced infinity, and there was light everywhere that he looked. There was not a shadow to be had, anywhere.

He seated himself in the nearest chair, and his reflection stared up at him from between his feet.

A prisoner of he who has already slain you once, he thought. No doubt near to his place of power, in a cage built just for me. Bad. Bad.

There was movement everywhere. The mirrors showed an instant's infinity of motion, then all was still once again. He looked about, seeking the result of this activity.

Beef, bread, wine and water now stood upon the table that hung above him.

Rising to his feet, he felt a light touch upon his shoulder. He turned quickly, and the Lord of Bats smiled at him and bowed.

"Dinner is served," he said, gesturing toward the table.

Jack nodded, moved with him, seated himself and began to fill his plate.

"How do you like your quarters?"

"I find them quite amusing," Jack replied. "I note an absence of doors and windows, among other things."

"Yes."

Jack began to eat. His appetite was like a flame that would not be quenched.

"Your journey has left you quite wretched-looking, you know."

"I know."

"I will have a bath sent around later, and some fresh garments."

"Thank you."

"No trouble. I want you to be comfortable during what will no doubt be a lengthy period of recuperation."

"How lengthy?" Jack inquired.

"Who knows? It could take years."

"I see."

If I were to attack him with the carving knife, Jack wondered, would I be able to kill him? Or would he be too strong for me now? Or able to summon his power in an instant? And if I were to succeed, could I find a way out of here?"

"Where are we?" Jack asked.

The Lord of Bats smiled.

"Why, we are right here," he said, touching his breast.

Jack frowned, puzzled.

"I do not—"

The Lord of Bats unfastened a heavy silver

chain he wore about his neck. A gleaming jewel hung suspended from it. He leaned forward and extended his hand.

"Study it for a moment, Jack," he said.

Jack touched it with his fingertips, weighed it, turned it.

"Well, would it be worth stealing?"

"Most likely. What sort of stone is it?"

"It is not actually a stone. It is this room. Consider the shape."

Jack did, shifting his eyes from the stone to the walls and back several times.

"Its shape is quite similar to that of this chamber . . ."

"It is identical. It must be, because they are the same thing."

"I fail to follow—"

"Take it. Hold it near to your eye. Consider its interior."

Jack raised it, closed one eye, squinted, stared.

"Inside . . ." he said. "There is a tiny replica of this chamber inside . . ."

"Look for this table."

"I see it! And I see us seated at it! I am—I am studying—This stone!"

"Excellent!" The Lord of Bats applauded.

Jack released it and the other raised it by its chain.

"Please observe," he said.

He moved his free hand toward it, enclosed the suspended gem in his fist.

There was darkness. It remained but a moment, departed as he loosened his grip.

Then he took a candle from beneath his cloak, wedged it into a hold in the table and struck a light to it. He swung the pendant near to the flame.

The chamber became warm, uncomfortably so. After a moment, the heat grew oppressive and Jack felt beads of perspiration begin upon his forehead.

"Enough!" he said. "There is no need to roast us!"

The other extinguished the flame and dipped the pendant into the water decanter. There came an immediate cooling.

"Where are we?" Jack repeated.

"Why, I wear us about my neck," said the Lord of Bats, replacing the chain.

"A good trick. Where are you now?"

"Here."

"Within the gem?"

"Yes."

"And you are wearing the gem."

"Obviously. Yes, it is a very good trick. It did not take me very long to work it out and to set it up. After all, I am undoubtedly the most capable of all the sorcerers—despite the fact that some of my most precious manuscripts dealing with the Art were stolen many years ago."

"What an unfortunate loss. I should think you would have guarded such documents most carefully."

"They were well-guarded. There was a fire, however. During the confusion, the thief was able to remove them and escape into the shadows."

"I see," said Jack, finishing a final piece of bread and sipping his wine. "Was the thief apprehended?"

"Oh yes. He was executed. But I am not finished with him yet."

"Oh?" said Jack. "What are your plans now?"

"I am going to drive him mad," said the Lord of Bats, swirling his wine within his goblet.

"Perhaps he is mad already. Is not kleptomania a mental disorder?"

The other shook his head.

"Not in this instance," he said. "With this thief it is a matter of pride. He likes to outwit the mighty, to appropriate their possessions. It seems to feed his self-esteem. If this desire is a mental disorder, then most of us suffer from it. In his case, though, the desire is often satisfied. He succeeds because he possesses some power and is shrewd and ruthless in its employment. I shall take great delight in observing his degeneration into a state of total madness."

"So as to feed your pride and self-esteem?"

"Partly. It will also constitute a bit of homage

to the god Justice and a benefit to society at large."

Jack laughed. The other only smiled.

"How do you intend to achieve the desired result?" he finally asked.

"I shall confine him to an inescapable prison where he will have absolutely nothing to do but exist. Occasionally, I will introduce certain items and remove them again—items which will come to occupy his thoughts more and more as time passes, inducing periods of depression and times of fury. I will break that smug self-assurance of his by rooting out the pride from which it grows."

"I see indeed," said Jack. "It sounds as if you have been planning this for a long while."

"Never doubt it."

Jack pushed away the empty platter, leaned back in the chair and considered the multitude of images that surrounded them.

"I daresay that the next thing you will tell me is that your pendant could accidentally be lost during an ocean voyage, buried, burnt or fed to hogs."

"I shan't, as it has already occurred to you."

The Lord of Bats rose to his feet, gestured casually toward a point high above their heads.

"I see that your bath has been drawn," he said, "and that fresh garments were laid out for you while we dined. I shall depart now and allow you to avail yourself of them."

Jack nodded, stood.

A thud occurred beneath the table then, followed by a gibbering sound and a brief, shrill wail. Jack felt his ankle seized. Then he was thrown to the floor.

"Down!" cried the Lord of Bats, circling the table quickly. "Back, I say!"

Scores of bats escaped his cloak and darted toward the thing beneath the table. It shrieked with fright and so tightened its grip upon Jack's ankle that he thought the bones would be pulverized.

He raised himself and began to lean forward. Then even the pain was insufficient to prevent a moment's paralysis from his revulsion at the sight he beheld.

The hairless member was white, shiny and blotched with blue marks. The Lord of Bats kicked it and the grip was broken; but before it drew away and moved to cross the other arm, shielding the face, Jack caught a glimpse of that lopsided countenance.

It looked like something that had started out to be a man but had never quite made it. It had been stepped on, twisted, had holes poked into the sickly dough of its head-bulge. Bones showed through the transparent flesh of its torso and its short legs were thick as trees, terminating in disk-shaped pads from which dozens of long toes hung like roots or worms. Its arms were longer than its entire body. It was a crushed slug, a thing that had been frozen and thawed before it was fully baked. It was—

"It is the Borshin," said the Lord of Bats, now extending his arms toward the squealing creature, which could not seem to decide whether it feared the bats or their Lord more, and which kept banging its head against the table's legs as it sought to avoid both.

The Lord of Bats tore the pendant from his neck and hurled it against the creature, uttering an oath as he did so. With this it vanished, leaving a small pool of urine werc it had crouched. The bats vanished within the dark one's cloak, and he smiled down at Jack.

"What," said Jack, "is a Borshin?"

The Lord of Bats studied his fingernails for a moment. Then, "For some time now the dayside scientists have," he said, "attempted to create artificial life. Thus far, they have not succeeded."

"I determined to succeed with magic where they had failed with their science," he went on. "I experimented for a long while, then made the attempt. I failed—or, rather, was only half-successful. You have just seen the results. I disposed of my dead homunculus in the Dung Pits of Glyve and one day that thing returned to me. I cannot take credit for its animation. The forces that restore us at that place stimulated it somehow. I do not believe the Borshin to be truly alive, in the ordinary sense of the word."

"Is it one of the items you mentioned, which will serve to torment your enemy?"

"Yes, for I have taught it two things: to fear me and to hate my enemy. I did not bring it here just now, however. It has its own ways of coming and going, though I did not think they extended to this place. I will have to investigate the matter further."

"In the meantime, it will be free to enter here whenever it chooses?"

"I am afraid so."

"Then might I borrow a weapon to keep with me?"

"I am sorry, but I have none to lend you."

"I see."

"I had best be going now. Enjoy your bath."

"One thing," said Jack.

"What is that?" asked the other, whose fingers were caressing the pendant.

"I, too, have an enemy for whom I contemplate an involved piece of vengeance. I will not bore you with details now, save that I believe mine will be superior to yours."

"Really? I would be interested to learn what you have in mind."

"I will see that you do."

Both smiled.

"Until later, then."

"Until later."

The Lord of Bats vanished.

Jack bathed, soaking himself for a long while in the lukewarm water. All the fatigue he had accumulated during his journey seemed to seize him then, and it took a mighty effort of will to rise, dry his body and walk to the bed, where he collapsed. He felt too tired to hate properly, or to begin planning his escape.

He slept, and while sleeping he dreamed.

He dreamed he held the Grand Key of Kolwynia, which was Chaos and Formation, and with it unlocked the sky and the earth, the sea and the wind, bidding them to fall upon High Dudgeon and its master from all corners of the world. He dreamt that there the flame was born and the dark Lord was held in its heart forever like an ant in amber, but alive, sleepless and feeling. Exulting in this, he heard the sudden chatter of the World Machine. He moaned and cried out at this omen; and within the walls, infinities of Jacks twisted on sweatdrenched beds.

5

JACK SAT IN the chair nearest the bed, his legs stretched out before him and crossed at the ankles, fingers interlaced beneath his chin. He wore the red, white and black diamond-patched clothing of a jester; his wine-colored slippers curled at the toes and ended in loose threads, where he had torn off the bells. He had discarded the quinopolus, and the belled cap had gone into the chamber pot.

Any moment now, he decided. I hope the Borshin does not follow him.

The remains of his thirty-first meal in that place, a breakfast, occupied the table. The air about him was cooler than he found comfortable. The Borshin had visited him on three occasions since his arrival, plumping into sudden existence, drooling and snatching at him. Each time, he had fended it off with a chair, while screaming as loudly as he could manage; and the Lord of Bats always followed after a few moments and drove the creature away, apologizing profusely for the inconvenience. Jack had been unable to sleep well since the first such visit, knowing that it could happen again at any time.

The meals appeared regularly, quite undistinguished repasts, and he ate them automatically while thinking of other matters. Afterward, he was never able to recall what they had featured, nor did he wish to.

Soon now he reflected.

He had exercised to keep from growing soft. He had gained back some of the weight he had lost. He had fought boredom by planning and rejecting many plots for escape and vengeance. Then Rosalie's words had returned to him, and he determined his course of action.

The air seemed to shimmer. There came a tone, not unlike the snapping of a fingernail against a goblet, somewhere near at hand.

Then the Lord of Bats was beside him, and this time he was not smiling.

"Jack," he began immediately, "you disappoint me. What were you attempting to establish?"

"I beg your pardon?"

"You just completed some sort of weak spell a few moments ago. Did you really think I would be unaware of a working of the Art here in High Dudgeon?"

"Only if it succeeded," said Jack.

"Which it obviously did not. You are still here."

"Obviously."

"You cannot shatter these walls, nor pass through them."

"So I've learned."

"Do you find time's weight increasing upon you?"

"Somewhat."

"Then perhaps it is time to introduce some additional element into your environment."

"You did not tell me there was another Borshin."

The other chuckled, and a bat emerged from somewhere, circled his head several times, suspended itself from the chain he wore.

"No, that is not what I had in mind," he said. "I wonder how much longer your sense of humor will hold up?"

Jack shrugged, rubbed idly at a smudge of soot on his right forefinger.

"Let me know when you find out," he said.

"I promise you will be among the first."

Jack nodded.

"I would appreciate it if you would refrain from further endeavors along magical lines," said the Lord of Bats. "In this highly charged atmosphere they could produce severe reper-cussions."

"I'll bear that in mind," said Jack.

"Capital. Sorry to have interrupted. I'll let you get back to your normal activities now. Adieu."

Jack did not reply, for he was alone.

It was some time later that the additional element appeared within his environment.

Realising that he was not alone, Jack looked up suddenly. At the sight of her coppery hair and her half-smile he was, for a moment, almost startled into believing.

Then he rose, moved toward her, moved to the side, studied her from several angles.

Finally, "It is a very good job," he said. "Give my compliments to your creator. You are an exceedingly fine simulacrum of my Lady Evene, of the Fortress Holding."

"I am neither a simulacrum nor am I your Lady," she said with a smile, curtseying.

"Whatever, you have brought me bright-ness," he said. "May I offer you a seat?"

"Thank you."

Seating her, he drew up another chair and set it to her left. Leaning back in it, he regarded her obliquely.

"Now will you riddle me your words?" he said. "If you are not my Evene nor a simulacrum

composed by my enemy to trouble me, then what
are you? Or—to be more delicate—who are you?"

"I am Evene of the Fortress Holding, daughter of Loret and the Colonel Who Never Died,"
she said, still smiling; and it was only then he
noticed that from the silver chain she wore
depended the strange gemstone that was shaped
in semblance of his chamber. "But I am not *your*
Lady," she finished.

"He did a very good job," said Jack. "Even
the voice is perfect."

"I can almost feel sorry for the vagabond
Lord of nonexistent Shadow Guard," she said,
"Jack of Liars. Being familiar with all forms of
baseness, it has become difficult for you to recognize the truth."

"There *is* a Shadow Guard!" he said.

"Then there is no need for you to grow
agitated at its mention, is there?"

"He taught you well, creature. To mock my
home is to mock me."

"That was my intention. But I am not a
creature of he whom you call the Lord of Bats.
I am his woman. I know him by his secret name.
He has shown me the world in a sphere. I have
seen all places and things from the halls of High
Dudgeon. I know that nowhere is there such a
place as Shadow Guard."

"No eyes but mine have ever looked upon
it," he said, "for it is always hidden by shadows.
It is a great, sprawling place, of high, torch-lit

halls, underground labyrinths and many towers. On the one hand it faces some light, and on the other the darkness. It is furnished with many mementos of the greatest thefts ever committed. There are things of great beauty there, and things of incalculable worth. The shadows dance in its corridors, and the facets of countless gems gleam brighter than the sun of the one-half world. That is the place you mock: Shadow Guard, next to which your master's keep is but a pigsty. It is sometimes, true, a lonely place; but the real Evene will brighten it with her laughter, touch it with her grace, so that it will endure in splendor long after your master has entered the final darkness as a result of my vengeance."

She applauded softly.

"You make it easy to recall how your words and your passion once persuaded me, Jack. I see now, though, that when you speak of Shadow Guard you speak too well to be describing a real place. I waited for you for a long while, and then I learned of your beheading at Iglés. Still, I was determined to await your return. But my father decided otherwise. At first, I believed his lust for the Hellflame ruled him. I was wrong, however. He realized from the first that you were a vagrant, a braggart, a liar. I wept when he bartered me for the Hellflame, but I came to love the one to whom I was given. My Lord is kind where you are thoughtless, intelligent where you are merely shrewd. His fortress really exists and is one of the mightiest in the land. He is all things that you are not. I love him."

Jack studied her now unsmiling face for a moment, then asked, "How did he come to possess the Hellflame?"

"His man won it for him in Iglés."

"What was that man's name?"

"Quazer," she said. "Quazer was champion of the Hellgames."

"A moderately useless piece of information for a simulacrum to possess," Jack observed, "if true. Yet, my enemy *is* of the fussy, thorough sort. I am sorry, but I do not believe you are real."

"It is an example of the egotism that blinds one to the obvious."

"No. I know that you are not the real Evene, but rather a thing sent to torment me, because the real Evene, my Evene, would have refrained from judging me in my absence. She would have waited for my answer to whatever was said against me."

She looked away then.

"More of your clever words," she finally said. "They mean nothing."

"You may go now," he said, "and tell your master you did not succeed."

"He is not my master! He is my Lord and lover!"

". . . Or you may stay, if you do not wish to go. It matters not at all."

He rose then, crossed to the bed, stretched out upon it, closed his eyes.

When he looked again, she was gone.

He had seen, however, that which she had not wished him to see.

. . . But I'll not give them anything, he decided. No matter what evidence they offer, I will explain it as a trick. I will keep my knowledge where I keep my feelings, for now.

After a time, he retreated into sleep, dreaming in bright colors of the future as he would have it.

He was left alone for a long while after that, which suited him perfectly.

He felt that he had held the Lord of Bats at bay, that he had defeated his first design upon his sanity. He occasionally chuckled as he paced the walls, ceilings, floors, surfaces of his chamber. He meditated upon his plan and its dangers, on the years that might be involved in achieving it. He ate his meals. He slept.

It occurred to him then that while at any given moment the Lord of Bats might be observing him, he could possibly be under observation at all times. He immediately had visions of the strange gemstone being passed from hand to hand by shifts of his enemy's servitors. The thought persisted. No matter what the action in which he was engaged, there came the nagging feeling that someone might be watching. He took to sitting for long spells glaring at possible watchers behind the mirrors. He would turn suddenly and gesture obscenely at invisible companions.

Gods! It's working! he decided one time, on awakening and looking quickly about the chamber. He *is* reaching! I suspect his presence everywhere, and it is beginning to unbalance me. But I've laid the groundwork. If he will just give me the opening I need and all other things remain as they are, I may have a chance. The best way to insure the opening, though, is to remain as untroubled-seeming as possible. I will have to stop pacing and watching, stop mumbling.

He lay there and opened his being and felt the sobering chill of the heights.

After that, he took to silence and slow movement. It was more difficult than he had thought to suppress his smaller reactions. But he suppressed them, sometimes seating himself, clasping his hands and counting through the thousands. The mirrors showed him that he wore a good-sized beard. His jester's garb grew worn and soiled. Often he would awaken in a cold sweat, unable to recall what nightmare had been tormenting him. Though his mind sometimes darkened, he now maintained the semblance of normalcy within his ever-lit prison of mirrors.

Is there a spell involved? he wondered. Or is it just the effects of prolonged monotony?

Probably the latter. I think I'd sense his spell, though he's a better magician than I. Soon now, soon. Soon he will be coming to me. He will feel that it is taking too long to distress me. There will come a counter-effect. *He* will be troubled. Soon, now. Soon he will come.

When he did, Jack had had advance notice.

He awakened to find a drawn bath—his second since his arrival, how many ages ago?—and a fresh costume. He scrubbed himself and donned the green-and-white garb. This time, he let the bells remain above his toes and he adjusted the cap to a rakish angle.

He seated himself then, clasped his hands behind his head and smiled faintly. He would not allow his appearance to betray the nervousness he felt.

When the air began to shimmer and he heard the note, he glanced in that direction and nodded slightly.

"Hello," he said.

"Hello," said the other. "How are you?"

"Quite recovered, I'd say. I should like to be taking my leave soon."

"In matters of health one cannot be too careful. I would say that you still require rest. But we shall discuss that matter at a later time.

"I regret that I have not been able to spend more time with you," he went on. "I have been occupied by matters which required my full attention."

"That is all right," said Jack. "All efforts will shortly come to nothing."

The Lord of Bats studied his face, as though seeking some sign of madness upon it. Then he seated himself and, "What do you mean?" he inquired.

Jack turned his left palm upward, and, "If all things end," he said, "then all efforts will come to nothing."

"Why should all things end?"

"Have you paid heed to the temperature recently, good my Lord?"

"No," said the other, perplexed, "I have not stirred physically from my keep for a long while."

"It might prove instructive for you to do so. Or, better yet, open your being to the emanations from the Shield."

"I shall—in private.—But there is always some leakage. The seven whose presences are required to dam it will learn of it and act. There is no cause for concern or foreboding."

"There is if one of the seven is confined and unable to respond."

The other's eyes widened.

"I don't believe you," he said.

Jack shrugged.

"I was seeking a safe place from which I might disembark when you offered me your— uh, hospitality. It is certainly easy enough to verify."

"Then why did you not speak of it sooner?"

"Why?" asked Jack. "If my sanity is to be destroyed, what is it to me whether the rest of the world goes on existing or is destroyed?"

"That is a very selfish attitude," said the Lord of Bats.

"It is *my* attitude," said Jack, and he jingled his bells.

"I suppose I must go check your story." The other sighed, rising.

"I'll wait here," said Jack.

The Lord of Bats led him into the high hall that lay beyond the iron door, and there he cut his bonds.

Jack looked about him. There were familiar designs worked in mosaics on the floor, heaps of rushes in the corners, dark hangings upon the walls, a small central altar with a table of instruments beside it, an odor of incense in the air.

Jack took a step forward.

"Your name was strangely entered in the book of Ells," said the Lord of Bats, "for that of another was blotted out above it."

"Perhaps the tutelary deity had second thoughts on the matter."

"To my knowledge, this has never occurred before. But if you are one of the seven chosen, so be it. Hear me, though, before you move to essay your part of the Shield duty."

He clapped his hands and a hanging stirred.

Evene entered the room. She went and stood at her Lord's side.

"While your powers may be necessary for this thing," he said to Jack, "do not think that they approach my own here in High Dudgeon. Soon we must strike lights, and there will be shadows. Even if I have underestimated you, know that my Lady has had years in which to study the Art and that she is uniquely gifted in its employment. She will add her skills to my own, should you attempt anything save that for which I brought you here. No matter what you believe, she is *not* a simulacrum."

"I know that," said Jack, "for simulacra do not weep."

"When did you see Evene weep?"

"You must ask her about it sometime."

She dropped her eyes as he turned his toward the altar and moved forward.

"I'd best begin. Please stand in the lesser circle," he said.

One by one, he ignited the charcoal within ten braziers, which stood in three rows of three, four and three each. He added aromatic powders, causing each to flame and cast smokes of different colors. Then he moved to the far side of the altar and traced a pattern upon the floor with the blade of an iron knife. He spoke softly and his shadow multiplied, recombined into one, swayed, grew still, darkened, and then stretched across the hall like an endless roadway to the east. It did not move thereafter, despite the flickering light, and grew so dark that it seemed to possess the quality of depth.

Jack heard the Lord of Bats' whispered, "I like this not!" to Evene, and he glanced in their direction.

Through the rolling smoke, by the flickering lights, within the circle, he seemed to take on a darker, more sinister appearance and to move with greater and greater assurance and efficiency. When he raised the small bell from the altar and rang it, the Lord of Bats cried, "Stop!" but he did not break the lesser circle as the sense of another presence, tense, watching, filled the hall.

"You are correct with respect to one thing," Jack said. "You are my master when it comes to the Art. I am not so addled as to cross swords with you, yet. Especially not in your place of power. Rather, I seek merely to occupy you for a time, to assure my safety. It will take even the two of you some minutes to banish the force I have summoned here—and then you will have other things to think about. Here's one!"

He seized a leg of the nearest brazier and hurled it across the hall. Its charcoal was scattered among rushes. They began to burn, and flames touched the fringes of a tapestry as Jack continued:

"I have not been summoned for Shield duty. With splinters from the table, charred in the

95

flame of our dinner candle, I altered the entry in the Book of Ells. Its opening unto me was the spell you detected."

"You dared break the Great Compact and tamper with the fate of the world?"

"Just so," said Jack. "The world is of little use to a madman, which is what you would have had me; and I spit on the Compact."

"You are henceforth and forever an outcast, Jack. Count no darksider as friend."

"I never have."

"The Compact and its agent, the Book of Ells, is the one thing we all respect—always have respected—despite all other differences, Jack. You will be hounded now to your ultimate destruction."

"I almost was, here, by you. This way, I am able to bid you good-bye."

"I will banish the presence you have summoned and extinguish the fire you have caused. Then I will raise half a world against you. Never again will you know a moment's rest. Your ending will not be a happy one."

"You slew me once, you took my woman and warped her will, you made me your prisoner, wore me around your neck, set your Borshin upon me. Know that when we meet again, I will not be the one who is tortured and hounded into madness. I have a long list, and you head it."

"We will meet again, Shadowjack—perhaps

even in a matter of moments. Then you can forget about your list."

"Oh, your mention of lists reminded me of something. Are you not curious as to whose name I effaced when I entered my own into the Book of Ells?"

"What name was it?"

"Strangely enough, it was your name. You should really get out more often, you know. If you had, you would have noticed the chill, inspected the Shield and read in the Book. Then you would have been on Shield duty and I would not have become your prisoner. All of this unpleasantness could have been avoided. There is a moral there somewhere. Get more exercise and fresh air—that may be it."

"In that case, you would have been the Baron's, or back in Glyve."

"A moot point," said Jack, glancing over his shoulder. "That tapestry is going pretty well now, so I can be moving along. In, say—perhaps a season, perhaps less—who knows?—whenever you finish your Shield duty—you will doubtless seek me. Do not be discouraged if you do not succeed at once. Persist. When I am ready, we will meet. I will take Evene back from you. I will take High Dudgeon away from you. I will destroy your bats. I will see you wander from offal to the grave and back again, many times. Good-bye, for now."

He turned away and stared along the length of his shadow.

"I will not be yours, Jack," he heard her say. "Everything I said before was true. I would kill myself before I would be yours."

He breathed deeply of the incensed air, then said, "We'll see," and stepped forward into shadow.

6

THE SKY LIGHTENED as, sack over shoulder, he trudged steadily eastward. The air was chill and snakes of mist coiled among gray grasses; valleys and gulches were filled with fog; the stars pierced a ghostly film of cloud; breezes from a nearby tarn lapped moistly at the rocky land.

Pausing for a moment, Jack shifted his burden to his right shoulder. He turned and considered the dark land he was leaving. He had come far and he had come quickly. Yet, farther must he go. With every step he took toward the light, his enemies' powers to afflict him were lessened. Soon, he would be lost to them. They would continue to seek him, however; they would not forget. Therefore, he did what must be done—he fled. He would miss the dark land, with its witcheries, cruelties, wonders and delights. It held his life, containing as it did the objects of his hatred and his love. He knew that he would have to return, bringing with him that which would serve to satisfy both.

Turning, he trudged on.

The shadows had borne him to his cache near Twilight, where he stored the magical documents he had accumulated over the years. He wrapped these carefully and bore them with him into the east. Once he achieved Twilight he would be relatively safe; when he passed beyond it, he would be out of danger.

Climbing, he worked his way into the Rennsial Mountains, at the point where the range lay nearest Twilight; there, he sought Panicus, the highest ridge.

Mounting above the mist, he saw the dim and distant form of Morningstar outlined against the Everdawn. There on his crag, couchant, unmoving, he faced the east. To one who did not know, he would have seemed a wind-sculpted pinnacle atop Panicus. Indeed, he was more than half of stone, his cat-like torso a solid thing joined with the ridge. His wings lay folded flat upon his back, and Jack knew—though he approached him from the rear—that his arms would still be crossed upon his breast, left over right, that the breezes had not disturbed his wire-like hair and beard, that his lidless eyes would still be fixed upon the eastern horizon.

There was no trail and the last several hundred feet of the ascent required the negotiation of a near-vertical face of stone. As always, for the shadows were heavy here, Jack strode up it as he would cross a horizontal plane. Before he reached the summit, the winds were screaming about him; but they did not drown out the voice of Morningstar, which rose as from the bowels of the mountain beneath him.

"Good morning, Jack."

He stood beside his left flank and stared high into the air, where Morningstar's head, black as the night he had left, was haloed by a fading cloud.

"Morning?" said Jack.

"Almost. It is always almost morning."

"Where?"

"Everywhere."

"I have brought you drink."

"I draw water from the clouds and the rain."

"I brought you wine, drawn from the grape."

The great, lightning-scarred visage turned slowly toward him, horns dipping forward. Jack looked away from the unblinking eyes whose color he could never remember. There is something awful about eyes which never see that which they were meant to look upon.

His left hand descended and the scarred palm lay open before Jack. He placed his wineskin upon it. Morningstar raised it, drained it, and dropped it at Jack's feet. He wiped his mouth with the back of his hand, belched lightly, returned his gaze to the east.

"What do you want, Shadowjack?" he asked.

"Of you? Nothing."

"Then why do you bring me wine whenever you pass this way?"

"You seem to like it."

"I do."

"You are perhaps my only friend," said Jack. "You have nothing that I wish to steal. I have nothing that you really need."

"It may be that you pity me, bound as I am to this spot."

"What is pity?" asked Jack.

"Pity is that which bound me here, to await the dawn."

"Then I'll have none of it," said Jack, "for I've a need to move around."

"I know. The one-half world has been informed that you have broken the Compact."

"Do they know why?"

"No."

"Do you?"

"Of course."

"How?"

"From the shape of a cloud I know that a man in a distant city will quarrel with his wife three seasons hence and a murderer will be hanged before I finish speaking. From the falling of a stone I know the number of maidens being seduced and the movements of icebergs on the other side of the world. From the texture of the wind I know where next the lightning will fall. So long have I watched and so much am I part of all things, that nothing is hidden from me."

"You know where I go?"

"Yes."

"And what I would do there?"

"I know that, too."

"Then tell me if you know, will I succeed in that which I desire?"

"You will succeed in that which you are about, but by then it may not be what you desire."

"I do not understand you, Morningstar."

"I know that, too. But that is the way it is with all oracles, Jack. When that which is foreseen comes to pass, the inquirer is no longer the same person he was when he posed the question. It is impossible to make a man understand what he will become with the passage of time; and it is only a future self to whom a prophecy is truly relevant."

"Fair enough," said Jack. "Only I am not a man. I am a darksider."

"You are all men, whatever side of the world you call home."

"I have no soul, and I do not change."

"You change," said Morningstar. "Everything that lives changes or dies. Your people are cold but their world is warm, endowed as it is with enchantment, glamourie, wonder. The lightlanders know feelings you will not understand, though their science is as cold as your people's hearts. Yet they would appreciate your realm if they did not fear it so and you might enjoy their feelings but for the same reason. Still, the capacity is there, in each of you. The fear need but give way to understanding, for you are mirror images of one another. So do not speak to me of souls when you have never seen one, man."

"It is as you said—I do not understand."

Jack seated himself upon a rock and, as did Morningstar, stared into the east.

After a time, "You told me that you wait here for the dawn," he said, "to see the sun rise above the horizon."

"Yes."

"I believe that you will wait here forever."

"It is possible."

"Don't you know? I thought you knew all things."

"I know many things, not all things. There is a difference."

"Then tell me some things. I have heard daysiders say that the core of the world is a molten demon, that the temperature increases as one descends toward it, that if the crust of the world be pierced then fires leap forth and melted minerals build volcanoes. Yet I know that volcanoes are the doings of fire elementals who, if disturbed, melt the ground about them and hurl it upward. They exist in small pockets. One may descend far past them without the temperature increasing. Traveling far enough, one comes to the center of the world, which is not molten—which contains the Machine, with great springs, as in a clock, and gears and pulleys and counterbalances. I know this to be true, for I have journeyed that way and been near to the Machine itself. Still, the daysiders have ways of demonstrating that their view is the correct one. I was almost convinced by the way one man explained it, though I knew better. How can this be?"

"You were both correct," said Morningstar. "It is the same thing that you both describe, although neither of you sees it as it really is. Each of you colors reality in keeping with your means of controlling it. For if it is uncontrollable, you fear it. Sometimes then, you color it incomprehensible. In your case, a machine; in theirs, a demon."

"The stars I know to be the houses of spirits and deities—some friendly, some unfriendly and many not caring. All are near at hand and can be reached. They will respond when properly invoked. Yet the daysiders say that they are vast distances away and that there is no intelligence there. Again . . .?"

"It is again but two ways of regarding reality, both of them correct."

"If there can be two ways, may there not be

a third? Or a fourth? Or as many as there are people, for that matter?"

"Yes," said Morningstar.

"Then which one is correct?"

"They all are."

"But to see it as it *is*, beneath it all! Is this possible?"

Morningstar did not reply.

"You," said Jack. "Have *you* looked upon reality?"

"I see clouds and falling stones. I feel the wind."

"But by them, somehow, you know other things."

"I do not know everything."

"But have you looked upon reality?"

"I—Once . . . I await the sunrise. That is all."

Jack stared into the east, watching the pink-touched clouds. He listened to falling stones and felt the wind, but there was no wisdom there for him.

"You know where I go and what I would do," he said, after a time. "You know what will happen, and you know what I will be like a long while from now. From up here on your mountain you can see all these things. You probably even know when I will die my final death and the manner of its occurrence. You make my life seem futile, my consciousness a thing that is merely along for the ride, unable to influence events."

"No," said Morningstar.

"I feel that you say this only so that I will not be unhappy."

"No, I say it because there are shadows across your life which I cannot pierce."

"Why can't you?"

"It may be that our lives are in some way intertwined. Those things which affect my own existence are always hidden from me."

"That's something, anyway," said Jack.

". . . Or it may be that, obtaining what you seek, you will place yourself beyond predictability."

Jack laughed.

"That would be pleasant," he said.

"Perhaps not so pleasant as you would think."

Jack shrugged.

"Whatever, I have no choice but to wait and see."

Far to his left and below—too far to hear its steady roar—a cataract plunged hundreds of feet and vanished from sight behind a rocky spur. Much farther below, a large stream meandered across a plain and wound its way through a dark forest. Farther still, he could see the smoke that rose above a village on its bank. For a moment, and without knowing why, he longed to walk through it, looking into windows and yards.

"Why is it," he asked, "that the Fallen Star who brought us knowledge of the Art, did not extend it to the daysiders as well?"

"Perhaps," said Morningstar, "the more theologically inclined among the lightlanders ask why he did not grant the boon of science to the darksiders. What difference does it make? I have heard the story that neither was the gift of the Fallen One, but both the inventions of man; that his gift, rather, was that of consciousness, which creates its own systems."

Then, panting and wheezing, with a great beating of dark green vanes, a dragon collapsed upon their shelf of stone. The wind had covered the sounds of its coming. It lay there, exhaling brief flames at a rapid rate. After a time, it rolled its apple-like red eyes upward.

"Hello, Morningstar," it said in silken tones. "I hope you do not mind my resting here a moment. Whoosh!" It exhaled a longer flame, illuminating the entire crag.

"You may rest here," said Morningstar.

The dragon noticed Jack, fixed him with his gaze, did not look away.

"I'm getting too old to fly over these mountains," it said. "But the nearest sheep are by that village on the other side."

Jack placed his foot within Morningstar's shadow as he asked, "Then why don't you move to the other side of the mountain?"

"The light bothers me," it replied. "I need

a dark lair." Then, to Morningstar, "Is it yours?" it said.

"Is what mine?"

"The man."

"No. He is his own."

"Then I can save myself a journey and clean your ledge for you as well. He is larger than a sheep, though doubtless less tasty."

Jack moved entirely within the shadow as the dragon exhaled a fountain of flames in his direction. These vanished as he inhaled, and Jack breathed them back at the dragon.

It snorted in surprise and beat with a pinion at its eyes, which suddenly watered. A shadow crept toward it then and fell across its face. This dampened a fresh attempt at incineration.

"You!" it said, glimpsing the shadow-garbed figure. "I thought you a twilighter come to trouble dear Morningstar. But now I recognize you. You are the infamous creature who pillaged my hoard! What did you do with my pale gold diadem of turquoise stones, my fourteen finely wrought silver bracelets, and my sack of moonbars which numbered twenty-seven?"

"Now they are a part of *my* hoard," said Jack, "and now you had best be going. Though you are larger than a piece of mutton, and doubtless less tasty, I may break my fast upon you."

He breathed another flame, and the dragon drew back.

"Desist!" said the dragon. "Give me leave to rest here but another moment, and I will depart."

"Now!" said Jack.

"You are cruel, shadow man." The dragon sighed. "Very well."

It stood, balancing its bulk with its long tail, then waddled and wheezed its way to the edge of the ridge. Glancing back, it said, "You are hateful," and then pushed itself over and was gone from sight.

Jack moved to the edge and watched it fall. When it seemed that it would be dashed to death upon the mountain's slope, its wings spread and caught the air; it rose then and glided in the direction of the village in the forest near the stream.

"I wonder as to the value of consciousness," said Jack, "if it does not change the nature of a beast."

"But the dragon was once a man," said Morningstar, "and his greed transformed him into what he is now."

"I am familiar with the phenomenon," said Jack, "for I was once, briefly, a pack-rat."

"Yet you overcame your passion and returned to manhood, as may the dragon one day. By virtue of your consciousness you recognized and overcame certain of those elements which made you subject to predictability. Consciousness tends to transform one. Why did you not destroy the dragon?"

"There was no need to," Jack began. Then he laughed. "It's carcass would have smelled up your cliff."

"Was it not that you decided that there was no need to kill that which you did not need to eat, or that which was no real threat to you?"

"No," said Jack, "for now I am just as responsible for the death of a sheep and depriving some village man of future meals."

It took Jack several seconds to recognize the sound which followed, a grinding, clicking noise. Morningstar was gnashing his teeth. A cold wind struck him then, and the light dimmed in the east.

". . . Perhaps you were right," he heard Morningstar saying softly, as though not addressing him, "about consciousness . . ." and his great, dark head was lowered slightly.

Uncomfortable, Jack looked away from him. His eyes followed the white, unblinking star which had always troubled him, as it moved on its rapid way from right to left in the east.

"The ruler of that star," he said, "has resisted all spells of communication. It moves differently from the others and faster. It does not twinkle. Why is this?"

"It is not a true star, but an artificial object placed into orbit above Twilight by the dayside scientists."

"To what end?"

"It was placed there to observe the border."

"Why?"

"Do they fear you?"

"We have no designs upon the lands of light."

"I know. But do you not also watch the border, in your own way?" asked Jack.

"Of course."

"Why?"

"To be aware of what transpires along it."

"That is all?" Jack snorted. "If that object is truly above Twilight, then it will be subject to magic as well as to its own laws. A strong enough spell will affect it. One day, I will knock it down."

"Why?" asked Morningstar.

"To show that my magic is superior to their science—for one day it will be."

"It would seem unhealthy for either to gain supremacy."

"Not if you are on the side that obtains it."

"Yet you would use their methods to enhance your own effectiveness."

"I will employ anything that serves my ends."

"I am curious as to what the result will be, ultimately."

Jack moved to the eastern edge of the pinnacle, swung himself over it, found a foothold, and looked upward.

"Well, I cannot wait here with you for the sun to rise. I must go chase it down. Good-bye, Morningstar."

"Good morning, Jack."

Like a peddler, sack upon his shoulder, he trudged toward the light. He moved through the smashed city of Deadfoot, not even glancing at the vine-webbed shrines of the useless gods, its most noted tourist attraction. Their altars never bore offerings worth stealing. Wrapping a scarf tightly about his head, he hurried up the famous Avenue of the Singing Statues. Each of these, noted individualists in life, commenced his own song at the sound of a footstep. Finally, after running (for it was a long thoroughfare), he emerged with temporary deafness, shortness of breath and a headache.

Lowering his fist, he halted in the middle of a curse, at a loss for words. He could think of no calamity to call down upon the deserted ruin which had not already been visited upon it.

When I rule, things will be different, he decided. Cities will not be planned so chaotically that they come to this.

Rule?

The thought had come unbidden into his head.

Well, why not? he asked himself. If I can obtain the power I seek, why not use it for everything that is desirable? After I have obtained my vengeance, I will have to come to terms with all those who are against me now. It might as well be as a conqueror. I am the only one who needs no fixed place of power. I shall be able to defeat the others on their own grounds once I hold the Key That Was Lost, Kolwynia. This thought must have been with me all along. I will reward Rosalie for having suggested the means.—And I must add to my list. After I have had my revenge upon the Lord of Bats, Benoni, Smage, Quazer and Blite, I will deal with the Baron and see that the Colonel Who Never Died has cause to change his name.

It amused him that, among others, he bore within his sack those very manuscripts which had aroused the Bat Lord's anger. For a time, he had actually considered the notion of offering to barter them for his freedom. The only reason he had not was the realization that the other would either accept and fail to release him, or—what would be worse—would keep the bargain. The necessity of returning stolen goods would be the greatest loss of face he had ever suffered. And this could only be expunged by doing what he was now doing: pursuing the power that would grant him satisfaction. Without the manuscripts, of course, this would be more difficult, and . . .

His head swam. He had been right, he decided, when he had spoken with Morningstar. Consciousness, like the noise of the double-hundred statues of Deadfoot, was a thing of discord and contradiction, giving rise to headaches.

Far to his right, the daysiders' satellite came into view once more. The world brightened as he moved forward. Smudges in distant fields, he saw the first beginnings of green ahead. The clouds burned more brightly in the east. The first bird song he had heard in ages reached his ears, and when he sought out the singer on its bough, he saw bright plumage.

A good omen, he decided later, to be met with song.

He stamped out his fire and covered it over, along with the bones and the feathers, before he continued toward day.

7

HE HAD FELT the beginnings of its slow approach at some point near to the middle of the semester. How, he was not certain. In this place, he seemed limited to the same sensory channels as his fellows. Still, groping, turning, hiding, correcting its passage, coming on again, it sought him. He knew that. As to its nature, he had no inkling. Recently, though, at times such as this, he felt that it was drawing near.

He had walked the eight blocks from the campus to The Dugout, passing high buildings with windows like slots in punch cards, moving along thoroughfares where, despite the passage of years, the exhaust from the traffic still came noxious to his nostrils. Turning, he had made his way up streets where beer cans rolled on the sidewalks and garbage spilled from the spaces between buildings. Passive-faced people, by windows, on stairs, in doorways, watched him as he walked. A passenger liner shattered the air high above him; from farther yet, the ever-unmoving sun sought to nail him, shadowless, to the hot pavement. Children at play about an opened fire hydrant had paused at their games to watch him as he went by. Then there had come the false promise of a breeze, the gurgling of the water, the hoarse complaint of a bird beneath some eaves. He had tossed his cigarette into the gutter and seen it swept on past him. All this light and I have no shadow, he thought. Strange how nobody's ever noticed. Where, precisely, did I leave it?

In places where lights were dim there was a change. It seemed to him that a certain quality either came into or departed the world. It was in the nature of an underlying sense of interconnectedness, which was not present in day's full glare. With it came small feelings and some impressions. It was as if, despite his deafness to them, the shadows still attempted to address him. It was in this way that he knew, upon entering the dark bar, that that which had been seeking him was now drawing near.

The heat of perpetual day dropped away as he moved to the rear of The Dugout. Touched here and there with auburn highlights, he saw her dark hair in the rosy glow of candle-light through glass. Threading his way among tables, he felt relaxed for the first time since he had left his class.

He slid into the booth across from her and smiled.

"Hi, Clare."

She stared, her dark eyes widening.

"John! You always do that," she said. "Suddenly you're just—there."

He continued to smile, studying her slightly heavy features, pinch marks where her glasses had been, a small puffiness beneath her eyes, some stray strands of hair reaching for her brow.

"Like a salesman," he said. "Here comes the waiter."

"Beer."

"Beer."

They both sighed, leaned back, and stared at one another.

Finally, she laughed.

"What a year!" she announced. "Am I glad this semester's over!"

He nodded.

"Largest graduating class yet."

"And the overdue books we'll never see . . ."

"Talk to someone in the front office," he said. "Give them a list of names—"

"The graduates will ignore billings."

"Someday they'll want transcripts. When they ask, hit them with notices that they won't be sent until they pay their fines."

She leaned forward.

"That's a good idea!"

"Of course. They'll cough up if it means a job to them."

"You missed your calling when you went into anthropology. You should have been an administrator."

"I was where I wanted to be."

"Why do you speak in the past tense?" she asked.

"I don't know."

"What's happened?"

"Nothing, really."

But the feeling was there. It was near.

"Your contract," she said. "Was there some sort of trouble?"

"No," he said. "No trouble."

The drinks arrived. He raised his and sipped it. Beneath the table, his leg brushed against hers as he crossed them. She did not move away; but then, she never did. From me or anyone else, thought Jack. A good lay, but too eager to get married. She's been impatient with me all semester. Any day now . . .

He dismissed the thoughts. He might have married her had he met her sooner, for he had no qualms about leaving a wife behind when he returned to where he must. But he had just met her this semester, and things were close to completion.

"What of the sabbatical you've been men-
tioning?" she asked. "Any decision on that yet?"

"I don't know. It depends on some research
I'm doing right now."

"How far along is it?"

"I'll know after I've used some computer
time I have coming."

"Soon?"

He glanced at his wristwatch and nodded.

"*That* soon?" she said. "If the indications are
favorable . . .?"

He lit a cigarette.

"Then it could be this coming semester," he
said.

"But you said that your contract was—"

"—in good order," he said. "But I didn't
sign it. Not yet."

"You once told me you thought Quilian
doesn't like you."

"He doesn't. He's old-fashioned. He thinks
I spend too much time with computers and not
enough in libraries."

She smiled.

"So do I."

"At any rate, I'm too popular a lecturer not
to be offered a renewal."

"Then why didn't you sign it? Are you asking
for more money?"

"No," he said. "But if I do ask for a sabbatical
and he refuses, it will be fun to tell him to shove
his contract. Not that I wouldn't sign one and

walk out, if it would benefit my—research. But I would enjoy telling Doc Quilian where to put his offer."

She sipped her beer.

"Then you must be near to something important."

He shrugged.

"How did your seminar wind up?" he asked.

She laughed.

"You certainly stick in Professor Weatherton's craw. He devoted most of the lecture to dismembering your Darkside Customs and Philosophies course."

"We disagree on many points, but he's never been darkside."

"He intimated that you haven't either. He agrees that it is a feudal society, and that some of its Lords may actually believe they possess direct control over everything in their realms. He dismisses the whole notion of their being loosely united in a Compact, based on a premise that the sky will fall if they do not maintain some sort of Shield by means of cooperating in magical endeavors."

"Then what keeps everything on that side of the world alive?"

"Somebody asked that question, and he said it was a problem for physical scientists, not social theorists. His personal opinion, though, was that it involved some sort of high altitude bleed-off from our force screens."

He snorted.

"I'd like to take him on a field trip sometime. His buddy Quilian, too."

"I know you've been darkside," she said. "In fact, I think your connection with it is even stronger than you say."

"What do you mean?"

"If you could see yourself now, you would know. It took me a long while to realize what it was, but when I noticed what gave you a strange appearance in places like this, it seemed obvious—it's your eyes. They are more light sensitive than any eyes I have ever seen before. As soon as you get out of the light and into a place like this, your pupils become enormous. There is only a faint line of color around them. And I noticed that the sunglasses you wear most of the time are far darker than ordinary ones."

"I do have an eye condition. They are quite weak, and bright lights irritate them."

"Yes, that's what I said."

He returned her smile.

He crushed out his cigarette, and as though this were a signal, a soft, sickening music slithered from out of a speaker set high on the wall above the bar. He took another drink of beer.

"I suppose Weatherton got in a few shots at the resurrection of bodies, too?"

"Yes."

And if I die here? he wondered. What will

become of me? Will I be denied Glyve and return?

"What's wrong?" she asked.

"What do you mean?"

"Your nostrils flared. Your brows contracted."

"You study features too much. It's that awful music."

"I like looking at you," she said. "But let's finish and go to my place. I'll play you something different. There is a thing I want to show you and ask you about, too."

"What is it?"

"I'd rather wait."

"All right."

They finished their drinks, and he paid. They departed, his feelings of apprehension subsiding as they moved into the light he filtered.

They climbed the stairs and entered her third-floor apartment. Just over the threshold, she halted and made a small noise in the back of her throat.

He pushed past her, moving quickly to the left. Then he halted.

"What is it?" he asked, searching the room with his eyes.

"I'm sure I didn't leave the place like this. Those papers on the floor . . . I don't think that chair was over there. Or that drawer opened. Or the closet door . . ."

He moved back to her side, studied the lock for scratches, found none. He crossed the room then, and she heard a sound that could only be the clicking of a knife blade as he entered the bedroom.

After a moment he emerged, vanished into the other room, passed from there into the bathroom. When he reappeared, he asked her, "Was that window by the table opened the way it is now?"

"I think so," she said. "Yes, I guess it was."

He sighed. He examined the windowsill, then said, "A gust of wind probably blew your papers. As for the drawer and the closet, I'd bet you left them open yourself this morning. And you've probably forgotten about moving the chair."

"I'm a very orderly person," she said, closing the door to the landing; and when she turned she said, "But I guess you're right."

"Why are you nervous?"

She moved about the apartment, picking up papers.

"Where did you get that knife?" she asked him.

"What knife?"

She slammed the closet door, turned and glared at him.

"The one you had in your hand a minute ago!"

He extended his hands, palms forward.

"I have no knife. You may search me if you wish. You will not find a weapon."

She moved to the chest of drawers, closed the one which had been opened. Stooping, she opened a lower one and removed a newsprint-wrapped parcel.

"This is a part of it," she said. "Why am I nervous? This is why!"

She placed the parcel on the table and undid the strings which held it.

He moved to her side and watched as she unwrapped the papers. Inside were three very old books.

"I thought you'd taken those back already!"

"I intended to—"

"That was the agreement."

"I want to know where you obtained them and how."

He shook his head.

"We also agreed that if I were to recover them, you would not ask me those questions."

She placed the books side by side, then pointed at the spine of one and the cover of another.

"I am certain those were not there before," she said. "They are bloodstains, aren't they?"

"I don't know."

"I tried to wipe some of the smaller ones off with a damp tissue. What came off certainly looked like dried blood."

He shrugged.

"When I told you these books had been stolen from their cases in the Rare Books Room and you offered to recover them, I said, 'Okay'." She continued, "I agreed that if you could get them back, I'd see that it was an anonymous return. No questions. But I never thought this meant bloodshed. The stains alone would not have made me think that that is what happened. But then I began considering you and realized how little I actually know. That's when I began noticing things like your eyes and the quiet way that you move. I had heard that you were friendly with criminals—but then you had written some articles on criminology and were teaching a course on the subject. So it seemed in order at the time I heard it. Now I see you move through my rooms with a knife in your hand, presumably ready to kill an intruder. No book is worth a human life. Our agreement is off. Tell me what you did to get them."

"No," he said.

"I must know."

"You staged that scene when we walked in here just to see what I'd do, didn't you?"

She blushed.

Now I suppose she'll try to blackmail me into marrying her, he thought, if she thinks she can make this thing big enough.

"All right," he said, jamming his hands into his pockets and turning to stare out the window. "I found out who did it and had a talk with him.

During the misunderstanding that followed, his nose got broken. He had the poor grace to bleed on the books. I couldn't get it all off."

"Oh," he heard her say; and then he turned and studied her face.

"That's all," he said.

He stepped forward then and kissed her. After a moment, she relaxed against him. For a time he massaged her back and shoulders, moved his hands to her buttocks.

Distraction complete, he decided, moving up along her rib cage and inward, slowly, toward the buttons of her blouse.

"I'm sorry." She sighed.

"That's all right," he said, unfastening them. "That's all right."

Later, while staring at a pillow through the curtain of her hair and analyzing his reactions to earlier events, he felt once again the nearing presence, this time so close that it almost seemed as if he were being watched. He glanced quickly about the room but saw nothing.

Listening to the sounds of traffic on the street below, he determined to be about his business soon, say in the space of a cigarette.

There came a sonic boom from overhead that rattled the window like a sudden hand.

Clouds, slowly gathering, obscured the sun somewhat. Knowing he was early, he parked his vehicle in the faculty lot and removed his heavy briefcase from the rear. The trunk of the car contained three heavy traveling bags.

He turned and began walking toward the far end of the campus. He felt a need to keep moving, to be ready to run if necessary. He thought of Morningstar at that moment, watching rocks and clouds and birds, feeling winds, rains, lightnings, and he wondered whether that one was instantly aware of every move he was making. He felt this to be so, and he wished that his friend were at hand to counsel him now. Did he know—or had he known for a long while—the outcome of what he was about to attempt?

The leaves and grasses had taken on that faint incandescence which sometimes precedes a storm. It was still quite warm, but now the heat was tempered by a light breeze from the north. The campus was almost deserted. He passed a group of students seated about the base of a fountain, comparing notes on an examination they had just taken. He thought he recognized two of them from his Introduction to Cultural Anthropology of several semesters back, but they did not look up as he went by.

As he passed Drake Hall, he heard his name called out.

"John! Doctor Shade!"

Halting, he saw the short, heavy figure of the young instructor Poindexter emerge from the doorway. The man's first name was also John, but since he had been a newcomer to their card group they had come to refer to him by his last name rather than confuse conversation.

Jack made himself smile as the man approached and nodded a greeting.

"Hi, Poindexter. I thought you'd be off recuperating by now."

"I still have some damn lab exams to grade," he said, breathing heavily. "I decided I wanted a cup of something hot, and the minute I closed the door to my office I knew what I'd done. The keys are on my desk and the door locks when it closes. There's nobody else in the building and the front office is shut down, too. I was standing there waiting for a guard to come by. I thought they might have access to a master key. Have you seen any guards?"

He shook his head.

"No, I just arrived a few moments ago. But I know the guards don't have access to masters.— Your office is on the far side of the building, isn't it?"

"Yes."

"I forget how high off the ground that would put it, but what about getting in through a window?"

"Too high, without a ladder—and they're both locked, anyhow."

"Let's go inside."

Poindexter ran the back of his hand across his ruddy forehead and nodded.

Entering and moving to the rear of the

building, he removed a ring of keys from his pocket and fitted one into the lock of the door Poindexter indicated. It turned, there was a click, and he pushed the door open.

"Lucky," he said.

"Where'd you get a master?"

"It's not a master, it's the key to my office. That's why you're lucky."

Poindexter's face opened into a yellowish smile.

"Thanks," he said. "Thanks a lot. Are you in a hurry?"

"No, I'm early for what I was about."

"Then let me get us something from the machine. I still want to take a break."

"All right."

He moved into the office, placed his briefcase behind the door, while the other's footsteps receded and were gone.

He stared out the window at the gathering storm. Somewhere a bell began to ring.

After a time, Poindexter returned and he accepted the steaming cup he proffered.

"How's your mother?"

"She's doing well. Should be out quite soon."

"Tell her I said hello."

"I will. Thanks. Nice of you to visit her."

They sipped at their cups, then, "It *is* lucky you came along," Poindexter said. "Maybe ours are the only two offices on campus with the same

130

lock. Hell, I would have settled for the ghost if he'd gotten me in."

"Ghost?"

"You know. The latest stunt."

"I'm afraid I haven't heard of it."

". . . A white thing, allegedly seen flitting around in trees and on the tops of buildings."

"When did this start?"

"Just recently, of course. Last semester it was mutagenic rocks in the Geology Building. The one before that, I think, it was aphrodisiacs in the water coolers. Same as always. A semester closes like the end of the world, I guess, full of portents and rumors. What's the matter?"

"Nothing. Have a cigarette."

"Thanks."

He heard a tiny bleat of thunder, and the ever-present odor from the laboratories aroused unpleasant memories. That's why I never liked this building, he realized. It's the smells.

"Will you be with us this coming semester?" Poindexter asked.

"I think not."

"Oh, you got your leave approved. Congratulations!"

"Not exactly."

A look of concern flashed at him through thick glasses.

"You're not quitting, are you?"

"It depends—on several things."

"If I may be selfish about it, I hope you decide to stay."

"Thanks."

"You'll keep in touch, though, if you do go?"

"Of course."

A weapon, he decided. I need something better than what I've got. But I can't ask him. It's good that I stopped in here, though.

He drew on his cigarette, glanced out the window. The sky had continued to darken; there appeared to be some moisture on the pane.

He gulped and dropped his cup into the wastebasket. Mashing out his cigarette, he stood.

"I'd better run if I'm going to make it to Walker before it starts to come down."

Poindexter stood and shook his hand.

"Well, if I don't see you again for a while, good luck," he said.

"Thanks.—The keys."

"What?"

"The keys. Why don't you take them off the desk and put them in your pocket now, just in case?"

Poindexter blushed and did it. Then he chuckled.

"Yes. I wouldn't want to do that again, would I?"

"I hope not."

He retrieved his briefcase while Poindexter lit the candles above his desk. There came a flash in the sky, followed by a low rumble.

"So long."

"Good-bye."

He departed and hurried to the Walker Buiding, pausing only to break into a laboratory and steal a bottle of sulfuric acid, taping the stopper in place.

8

HE TORE OUT the first pages of the print-out and spread them on the table he had appropriated. The unit continued its clicking, drowning out the sounds of the rain.

He returned to the machine, tore out the next page. He placed it beside the others and regarded them.

There came a sound like scratching from the direction of the window, and he jerked his head upright, nostrils dilated.

Nothing. There was nothing there.

He lit a cigarette and dropped the match on the floor. He paced. He checked his wristwatch. A candle flickered above its sconce and the wax slid down its side. He moved to the window and listened to the wind.

There came a click from the door, and he

turned and faced it. A large man entered the room and regarded him. He removed a dark rain hat, placed it on the chair beside the door, ran a hand through his thin, white hair.

"Docor Shade," he said, nodding and unbuttoning his coat.

"Doctor Quilian."

The man hung his coat beside the door, produced a handkerchief and began wiping his glasses.

"How are you?"

"Fine, thank you. Yourself?"

"Fine."

Dr. Quilian closed the door, and the other returned to the machine and tore out more pages.

"What are you doing?"

"Some figuring for that paper I told you about—a couple of weeks ago, I guess."

"I see. I just recently learned about your arrangement here." He gestured toward the machine. "Whenever anyone cancels out, you're right there to take over his computer time."

"Yes. I keep in touch with everyone on the roster."

"There have been an awful lot of cancellations recently."

"I think it's the flu."

"I see."

He drew on his cigarette. He dropped it and stepped on it when the machine stopped printing. Turning, he removed the final print-outs. He took them to the table where the others lay.

Dr. Quilian followed him.

"May I see what you've got there?" he inquired.

"Surely," he said, and offered him the papers.

After a moment, "I don't understand them," said Quilian.

"If you had, I would have been very surprised. They're about three times removed from reality, and I'll have to translate them for my article."

"John," said the other, "I'm beginning to have some funny feelings about you."

The other nodded and lit another cigarette before he recovered the print-outs.

"If you want the computer yourself, I'm finished now." he said.

"I've been thinking a lot about you. How long have you been with us?"

"Around five years."

There came a sound from the window once more, and they both turned their heads.

"What was that?"

"I don't know."

After a time, "You get to do pretty much what you want to around here, John . . ." said Quilian, adjusting his glasses.

"That's true. I appreciate it."

"You came to us with good-seeming credentials, and you've proven to be quite an expert on darkside culture."

"Thank you."

"I didn't exactly mean it as a compliment."

"Oh, really?" He began to smile as he studied the final page of the print-out. "What *do* you mean?"

"I've got a strange feeling you've misrepresented yourself, John."

"In what way?"

"On your application for a position here, you stated that you were born in New Leyden. There is no record of your birth in that city."

"Oh? How did this come to light?"

"Doctor Weatherton was up that way recently."

"I see. Is that all?"

"Outside of the fact that you are known to keep company with hoodlums, there is some doubt as to the validity of your degree."

"Weatherton again?"

"The source is unimportant. The conclusion is not. I do not feel that you are what you purport to be."

"Why choose tonight, here, to air your doubts?"

"The semester's over, I know that you want to go away, and tonight was your last session with the machine—according to the time you

137

applied for. I want to know what you are taking away with you and where you are taking it."

"Carl," he said, "what if I admitted that I did misrepresent myself a bit? You've already stated that I'm an expert in my area. We both know I'm a popular lecturer. Whatever Weatherton dug up—What of it?"

"Are you in some kind of trouble, Jack? Something I might be able to help you with?"

"No. Not really. No trouble."

Quilian crossed the room and seated himself on a low couch.

"I've never seen one of you this close before," he said.

"What are you implying?"

"That you are something other than a human being."

"Like what?"

"A darkborn. Are you?"

"Why?"

"They are supposed to be taken into custody, under certain conditions."

"I take it that if I am, those conditions will be deemed to have been met?"

"Perhaps," said Quilian.

"And perhaps not? What do you want?"

"For now, all that I want is to know your identity."

"You know me," he said, folding the pages and reaching for his briefcase.

Quilian shook his head.

"Of the things about you which trouble me," he said, "I've just recently found a new one which gives me considerable cause for concern. Allowing for a moment that you are a darksider who has emigrated into day, there are certain correspondences which force me to pursue the question of your identity. There is a person whom I had considered possessed only of a mythological existence, on the darkside of the world. I wonder, would the legendary thief dare to walk in sunlight? And if so, for what reason? Could Jonathan Shade be the mortal equivalent for Jack of Shadows?"

"And what if it is?" he asked, striving to keep his eyes from moving to the window, where something seemed now to be occluding much of the dim light. "Are you prepared to place me under arrest?" he asked, moving slowly to his left so that Quilian would turn his head to follow.

"Yes, I am."

He glanced toward the window himself then, and an old loathing returned to him as he saw what was pressed against it.

"Then I take it that you have come armed?"

"Yes," he said, removing a small pistol from his pocket and pointing it.

I could throw the briefcase and risk taking one round, he decided. After all, it's a small enough weapon. Still, if I buy time and get closer to the light, it may not be necessary.

"It is strange that you came alone, if you

had such a thing in mind. Even if you do have the authority to make a security arrest on campus—"

"I did not say that I am alone."

"—Not really strange, though, now that I think of it." He took a step nearer the flickering light. "*I* say that you are alone. You would like to handle this yourself. It may simply be that you wish to kill me without witnesses. Or it may be that you desire full credit for my apprehension. I'd guess the former, though, because you seem to dislike me very much. Why, I'm not certain."

"I fear that you overestimate your ability to create a disliking, as well as my own for violence. —No, the authorities have been notified and an arresting party is on its way here. My intention is only to require your presence until they arrive."

"It would seem that you waited until about the last possible moment."

With his free hand, Quilian gestured toward the briefcase.

"I've a suspicion that once your latest project has been deciphered, it will be found to have little to do with the social sciences."

"You are a very suspicious person. There are laws against arresting people without evidence, you know."

"Yes, that's why I waited. I'm betting that's evidence that you are holding—and I am certain

140

that more will turn up. I have noted, too, that when it comes to matters of security the laws are considerably relaxed."

"You do have a point there," he replied, turning so that the light caught him full in the face.

"I am Jack of Shadows!" he cried out. "Lord of Shadow Guard! I am Shadowjack, the thief who walks in silence and in shadows! I was beheaded in Igles and rose again from the Dung Pits of Glyve. I drank the blood of a vampire and ate a stone. I am the breaker of the Compact. I am he who forged a name in the Red Book of Ells. I am the prisoner in the jewel. I duped the Lord of High Dudgeon once, and I will return for vengeance upon him. I am the enemy of my enemies. Come take me, filth, if you love the Lord of Bats or despise me, for I have named myself Jack of Shadows!"

Quilian's face showed puzzlement at this outburst, and though he opened his mouth and tried to speak, his words were drowned out by the other's cries.

Then the window shattered, the candle died, and the Borshin sprang into the room.

Turning, Quilian saw the gashed, rain-drenched thing across the room. He let out an incoherent cry and stood as if paralyzed. Jack dropped his briefcase, found the vial of acid and unstoppered it. He hurled its contents at the creature's head, and without pausing to observe the results, he snatched up his briefcase and dodged past Quilian.

He was to the door before the creature let out its first shriek of pain. He passed into the hallway, locking the door behind him, having paused only sufficiently to steal Quilian's raincoat from where it was hanging.

He was halfway down the building's front steps when he heard the first shot. There were others, but he was crossing the campus when they came, clutching the raincoat about his shoulders and cursing the puddles, and so he did not hear them. Besides, there was thunder. Soon, he feared, there would be sirens too.

Thinking stormy thoughts, he ran on.

The weather assisted him in some ways, hindered him in others.

What traffic there was had been slowed down considerably, and when he reached a stretch of open road, its long dry surface had become sufficiently slippery to preclude his moving at the speeds he desired. The darkness of the storm was causing motorists to depart from the streets at the first opportunity, as well as keeping those already home where they were, safe in the glow of many candles. There were no pedestrians in sight. All of which made it easy for him to abandon his vehicle and appropriate another before he had gone very far.

Getting out of town was not difficult, but

outrunning the storm was another matter. They both seemed headed in the same direction: one of the routes he had mapped out and memorized long ago as both expeditious and devious in returning him to darkness. On any other occasion he would have welcomed a diminution in that constant glare which had first burned, then tanned his unwilling hide. Now, it slowed him, and he could not risk an accident at this point. It bathed the vehicle, and its winds caused it to sway, while its bolts of lightning showed him the skyline he as leaving.

Police lanterns set on the road caused him to slow apprehensively, seeking exit from the highway. He sighed and grinned faintly as he was waved on by the scene of a three-car accident, where a man and woman were being borne on stretchers toward a gaping ambulance.

He played with the radio but obtained only static. He lit a cigarette and opened the window partway. An occasional droplet struck against his cheek, but the air was cool and sucked the smoke away. He breathed deeply and attempted to relax, having just realized how tense he had been.

It was not until considerably later that the storm slowed to a steady drizzle and the sky began to lighten somewhat. He was driving through open country at that point and feeling a mixed sense of relief and apprehension which had grown between curses since his departure.

What have I accomplished? he asked himself, thinking back over the years he had spent dayside.

It had taken considerable time for him to familiarize himself with the areas involved, obtain the necessary credentials, and learn the teaching routine. Then came the matter of finding employment at a university possessing the necessary data-processing facilities. In his spare time, he had had to learn to use the equipment, then conceive projects which would allow him to do so without question. Then he had had to review everything he possessed in the way of primary data with respect to his real questions, organize the information, and cast it into the proper form. The entire process had taken years, and there had been failures, many of them.

This time, though, this time he had been so near that he could taste it, smell it. This time he had known that he was close to the answers he had been seeking.

Now, he was running away with a briefcase full of papers he had not had an opportunity to review. It was possible that he had failed again and was returning without the weapon he had sought, returning to the place of his enemies. If this were the case, he had only postponed his doom. Still, he could not remain—for here, too, he had acquired enemies. He wondered briefly whether there was some cryptic lesson involved, some available but overlooked insight that would show him more about himself than about his enemies. If so, it eluded him.

Just a little longer . . . If he had only had a bit more time, he could have checked, then reformulate and reprogrammed if necessary. Now there was no more time. There could be no going back to hone it if it was a blunted sword he bore. And there were other matters, personal ones, he had wished to draw to better conclusions. Clare, for instance . . .

Later, the rain let up, though the cloud-cover remained total and threatening. He risked speeding then and tried the radio once more. Bursts of static still occurred, but there was more music than there was interference, so he let it play.

When the news came on, he was winding his way down a steep hill, and while he thought that he heard his name spoken, the volume had diminished too much for him to be certain. Alone on the road at that point, he began looking back over his shoulder regularly and up every side way he passed. It infuriated him that the mortals still had a fair chance of apprehending him before he achieved a situation of power. Ascending a higher hill, he saw a curtain of rain far off to his left and a few feeble flickers of lightning, so distant that he heard no following thunder. Continuing his search of the heavens, he saw that they were barren of traffic and he thanked the Storm King for that. Lighting a fresh cigarette, he brought in a stronger station, waited for the news. When it came, there was no report concerning himself.

He thought of the distant day when he had stood beside a rainpool and discussed his plight with his reflection there. He tried to see that dead self now—tired, thin, cold, hungry, sore-footed and smelling badly. All of the irritants were erased, except a small hunger just beginning in his middle and hardly worth comparison with those earlier feelings, which were near starvation. Still, how dead was that old self? How had his situation been altered? Then, he had been fleeing from the West Pole of the World, striving to keep alive, trying to evade pursuers and reach Twilight. Now, it was the bright East Pole from which he fled, toward Twilight. Driven by hatred and something of love, revenge had been hot in his heart, warming him and feeding him. Nor was it absent now. He had acquired knowledge of dayside arts and sciences, but this in no way changed the man who had stood beside the pool; he stood there still, within him, and their thoughts were the same.

"Morningstar," he said, opening the window and addressing the sky, "since you hear everything, hear this: I am no different than when last we spoke."

He laughed. "Is that good or bad?" he asked, the thought just occurring to him. He closed the window and considered the question. Not fond of introspection, he was nevertheless inquisitive.

He had noted changes in people during his stay at the university. It was most apparent in the students, and it occurred in such a brief time —that short span between matriculation and graduation. However, his colleagues had also altered in small ways which involved attitudes and sentiments. He alone had not changed. Is this something fundamental? he wondered. Is this part of the basic difference between a daysider and a darksider? They change and we do not. Is this important? Probably, though I do not see how. We have no need to change, and it seems that they do. Why? Length of life? Different approach to life? Possibly both. What value is there in change, anyway?

He turned off onto a seemingly deserted side road after the next news broadcast. This one had named him as wanted for questioning in connection with a homicide.

Into the small fire he kindled, he tossed every piece of identification that he carried. While they burned, he opened his bag and refilled his wallet with fresh papers he had prepared several semesters earlier. He stirred the ashes and scattered them.

Carrying it across a field, he tore Quilian's raincoat in several places and tossed it into a gully where muddy waters rushed. Returning to the vehicle, he decided to trade it for another before very long.

Hurrying up the highway then, he reflected on the situation as he now understood it. The Borshin had killed Quilian and departed, doubtless as it had come, through the window. The reason for Quilian's presence there was known to the authorities, and Poindexter would verify his own presence on campus and his stated destination. Clare, and many others, could testify as to their disliking one another. The conclusion was obvious. Though he would have killed Quilian had the necessity arisen, he grew indignant at the thought of being executed for something he had not done. The situation reminded him of what had occurred at Iglés, and he rubbed his neck half-consciously. The unfairness of it all smarted.

He wondered whether the Borshin in its frenzy of pain had thought it was slaying him or was merely acting to defend itself, knowing that he had escaped. How badly injured was it: He knew nothing of the creature' recuperative abilities. Was it even now seeking his trail, which it had followed for so long? Had the Lord of Bats sent it to find him, or was it following its own feelings, conditioned as it was to hate him? Shuddering, he increased his speed.

Once I'm back, it won't matter, he told himself.

But he wondered.

He obtained another vehicle on the far side of the next town he passed through. In it, he hurried toward Twilight, near the place where the bright bird had sung.

For a long while he sat on the hilltop cross-legged, reading. His clothing was dusty and there were rings of perspiration about the armpits; there was dirt beneath his fingernails, and his eyelids had a tendency to droop, close, spring open again. He sighed repeatedly and made notes on the papers he held. Faint stars shone above the mountains to the west.

He had abandoned his final vehicle many leagues to the east of his hilltop, continuing then on foot. It had been stalling and knocking for some time before it stopped and would not start again. Knowing then that he had passed the place where the rival Powers held truce, he stumbled on toward the darkness, taking only his briefcase. High places always suited him best. He had slept but once on his journey; and while it had been a deep, sound, dreamless sleep, he had begrudged his body every moment of it and vowed not to do it again until he had passed beyond the jurisdiction of men. Now that he had done so, there was but one thing more before he would allow himself to rest.

Scowling, he turned the pages, located what he sought, made a marginal notation, returned to the place of the original markings.

It seemed to be right. It seemed almost to fit . . .

A cool breeze crossed the hilltop, bringing with it wild scents that he had all but forgotten in the cities of men. Now it was the stark light of the Everyday, not the smells and noises of the city, not the files and ranks of faces in his classrooms, not the boring meetings, not the monotonous sounds of machinery, not the obscene brightness of colors that seemed a receding dream. These pages were its only token. He breathed the evening, and the back translation he had made from the print-out leaped toward his eyes and quickened within his mind like a poem suddenly understood.

Yes!

His eyes sought the havens and found the white, unblinking star that coursed them.

He rose to his feet with his fatigue forgotten. With his right foot he traced a brief pattern in the dirt. Then he pointed a finger at the satellite and read the words that he had written upon the papers he held.

For a moment nothing happened.

Then it stood still.

Silent now, he continued to point. It grew bright and began to increase in size.

Then it flared like a shooting star and was gone.

"A new omen," he said and then smiled.

9

WHEN THE DAMNED thing entered High Dudgeon, it swept from chamber to chamber in search of its Lord. When it located him at last, casting sulfur into a pool of mercury in the center of an octagonal room, it obtained his attention and suspended itself from the outstretched finger he offered. It conveyed to him then, in its own fashion, the news that it had borne.

With this he turned, performed a curious act involving a piece of cheese, a candle and a feather and departed the chamber.

He removed himself to a high tower and for a long while there regarded the east. Quickly then, he turned and studied the only other avenue in his keep—the westnorth.

Yes, there too! But it was impossible.

Unless, of course, it was an illusion . . .

He mounted a stair that wound widdershins about the wall, opened a trapdoor, and climbed outside. Raising his head, he studied the great black orb bright stars all about it; he sniffed the wind. Looking downward, he regarded the massive, sprawled keep that was High Dudgeon, raised by his own power shortly after his creation upon this mountaintop. When he had learned the difference between the created and the born and had discovered that his power was centered at this point in space, he had sucked power up into him through the roots of the mountain and drawn it down in a whirlwind from the heavens, so that he had glowed, dazzling, like a struck lightning rod, and engaged in creation himself. If his power resided here, then this place was to be his home, his fortress. And so it was. Those who would do him ill had died and so had learned their lessons, or they darted the Everdark on leathery wings till they earned his favor. The latter he saw sufficiently well-tended so that upon their release into the manform, many had elected to remain in his service. The other Powers, perhaps as strong as he in their own ways, in their own spheres, had troubled him little once suitable boundaries had been established.

For anyone to move against High Dudgeon now . . . It was unthinkable! Only a fool or a madman would attempt such a thing.

Yet now there were mountains where no

mountains had been—mountains, or the appearance of mountains. He raised his eyes from his home and studied the distant shapes. It troubled him that he had been unable to detect within his person the existence of such a welling of forces as would be necessary to create even the appearance of mountains within his realm.

Hearing a footstep on the stair, he turned. Evene emerged from the opening, mounted above it, and moved to his side. She wore a loose, black garment, short-skirted, belted at the waist, and clasped at her left shoulder with a silver brooch. When he put his arm about her and drew her to him, she trembled, feeling the currents of power rising in his body; she knew that he would not favor speaking.

He pointed at the mountain he faced, then at the other, to the east.

"Yes, I know," she said. "The messenger told me. That is why I hurried here. I've brought you your wand."

She raised the black, silken sheathe she bore at her girdle.

He smiled and moved his head slightly from left to right.

With his left hand, he raised and drew off the pendant and chain he wore about his neck. Holding it high, he dangled the bright gem before them.

She felt a swirling of forces and seemed for

an instant to be falling forward into the stone. It grew, filling her entire field of vision.

Then it was no longer the jewel, but the sudden westnorth mountain that she beheld. For a long while, she stared at the high gray-and-black dome of stone.

"It looks real," she said. "It seems so—substantial."

Silence.

Then, as star by star, the lights in the sky vanished behind its peaks, its shoulders, its slopes, she exclaimed, "It—it's growing!" and then, "No . . . It's moving, moving toward us," she said.

It vanished, and she stared at the pendant as it had been. Then he turned, turning her with him, and they faced the east.

Again the swirling, the falling, the growing.

Now the eastern mountain, its face like the prow of a great, strange ship, lay before them. Cold lights lined its features and it, too, plowed the sky, advancing. As they watched, high wings of flame rose behind it and flashed before it.

"There is someone upon—" she began.

But the jewel shattered and the chain, glowing sudden red with heat, fell from her Lord's hand. It lay smoking at their feet. She received a sudden shock from his body as this occurred, and she pulled away from him.

"What happened?"

He did not reply, but extended his hand.

"What is it?"

He pointed at the wand.

She handed it to him and he raised it. Silently, he summoned his servants. For a long while he stood so, and then the first appeared. Soon they swarmed about him, his servants, the bats.

With the tip of his wand he touched one, and a man fell at his feet.

"Lord!" cried the man, bowing his head. "What is thy will?"

He pointed toward Evene, until the man raised his eyes and turned his head toward her.

"Report to Lieutenant Quazer," she said, "who will arm you and assign you duties."

She looked at her Lord and he nodded.

With his wand then, he began touching the others, and they became what they once had been.

An umbrella of bats had spread above the tower, and a seemingly endless column of larger creatures filed past Evene, down the stairway and into the keep below.

When all had passed, Evene turned toward the east.

"So much time has gone by," she said. "Look how much closer the thing has come."

She felt a hand upon her shoulder and, turning, she raised her face. He kissed her eyes and mouth, then pushed her from him.

"What are you going to do?"

He pointed toward the trapdoor.

"No," she said. "I won't go. I will stay and assist you."

He continued to point.

"Do you know what it is that's out there?"

"Go," he had said, or perhaps she only thought that he had said it. She recalled it, standing within her chamber at the eastsouth edge of the keep, uncertain as to what had occurred since the word had filled her mind and body. She moved to the window and there was nothing to see but stars.

But suddenly, somehow, then, she knew.

She wept for the world they were losing.

They were real, he knew that now. For they crushed as they came, and he felt the vibrations of their movements within his body. While the stars told him that a bad time was at hand—a long, bad time—he did not require their counsels to this end. He continued to draw upon the forces which had raised High Dudgeon and were now to defend it. He began to feel as he had in that distant time.

On the peak of the new mountain to the east, a serpent began to form. It was of fire, and he could not guess at its size. In the times before his time, such Powers were said to have existed. But the wielders had passed to their final deaths and the Key had been lost. He had sought it himself; most of the Lords had. Now it appeared that another had succeeded where he had failed—that, or an ancient Power was stirring once more.

He watched the serpent achieve full existence. It was a very good piece of work, he decided. He watched it rise into the air and swim toward him.

Now it begins, he said to himself.

He raised his wand and began the battle.

It was a long while before the serpent fell, gutted and smoking. He licked at the perspiration which had appeared upon his upper lip. The thing had been strong. The mountain was closer now; its movement had not slowed while he had battled the thing sent against him.

Now, he decided, I must be as I was in the beginning.

Smage paced his post, the forward entrance hall to High Dudgeon. He paced as slowly as he could, so as not to betray his uneasiness to the fifty-some warriors who awaited his orders. Dust fell about him, rose again. There would be startled movements among those of his command whenever a weapon or piece of armor, dislodged from its place on a wall, would crash to the floor somewhere within the keep. He glanced through a window and looked quickly away; everything without had been blotted from sight by the bulk which stood now at hand. There came a constant rumbling, and unnatural cries would pierce the darkness. Lightninglike, apparitions of headless knights, many-winged birds and man-headed beasts passed before his eyes and faded, as well as things which left no forms within his memory; yet none of these paused to menace him. Soon now, soon it would be over, he knew, for the prow of the mountain must be nearing his Lord's tower.

When the crash came, he was thrown from his feet, and he feared that the hall would collapse upon him. Cracks appeared in the walls, and the entire keep seemed to move backward a pace. There came the sounds of falling masonry and splintering beams. Then, after several heart-beats, he heard a scream high overhead, followed by a final crashing note somewhere in the court-yard to his left. This was followed by dust and silence.

He rose to his feet and called for his troop to assemble.

Wiping the dust from his eyes, he looked about him.

They were all of them on the floor and none of them moving.

"Arise!" he cried; and he rubbed his shoulder.

After another moment of stillness, he moved to the nearest and studied the man. He did not seem to be injured. He slapped him lightly, and there was no reaction. He tried another; he tried two more. It was the same. They seemed barely to breathe.

Unsheathing his blade, he moved toward the courtyard to his left. Coughing, he entered it.

Half the firmament was shadowed by the now motionless mountain, and the courtyard held the ruins of the tower. Its prow had broken. The present stillness seemed more terrible than the earlier rumbling and the recent din. The apparitions all had vanished. Nothing stirred.

He moved forward. As he advanced, he saw blastmarks, as though lightning had played about the place.

He halted when he saw the outstretched figure at the edge of the rubble. Then he rushed forward. With the point of his blade, he turned the body.

He dropped the blade and fell to his knees, gripping the mangled hand to his breast, a single sob escaping his throat. He heard the crackling of fires begin suddenly at his back, and he felt a rush of heat. He did not move.

He heard a chuckle.

He looked up then, looked all about him. But he saw no one.

It came again, from somewhere to his right. There!

Among the shadows that moved on the slanting wall . . .

"Hello, Smage. Remember me?"

He squinted. He rubbed his eyes.

"I—I can't quite make you out."

"But I see you perfectly there, clutching the meat."

He lowered the hand gently and raised his blade from the flagging. He stood.

"Who are you?"

"Come find out."

"You did all this?" He made a small gesture with his free hand.

"All."

"Then I will come."

He advanced upon the figure and swung his blade. It cut but air, throwing him off balance. Recovering, he aimed another blow. Again, there was nothing.

He wept after his seventh attempt.

"I know you now! Come out of those shadows and see how you fare!"

"All right."

There was movement, and the other stood before him. He seemed for a moment tall beyond measurement, frightening, noble.

Smage's hand hesitated upon the blade, and the hilt took fire. He released it, and the other smiled as it fell between them.

He raised his hands and a paralysis overcame them. Through fingers like twisted boughs he regarded the other's face.

"As you suggested," he heard him say. "And I seem to be faring well. Better than yourself certainly.

"I'm pleased to meet you once again," he added.

Smage wished to spit, but he could summon no saliva; besides, his hands were in the way.

"Murderer! Beast!" he croaked.

"Thief," the other said gently. "Also, sorcerer and conqueror."

"If I could but move—"

"You will. Pick up your blade and cut me your carrion's toenails—behind the neck, of course."

"I do not . . ."

"Lop off the head! Let it be done with one, quick, clean blow—as by a headsman's axe."

"Never! He was a good Lord. He was kind to me and my comrades. I will not defile his body."

"He was not a good Lord. He was cruel, sadistic."

"Only to his enemies—and they had always earned it."

"Well, now you see a new Lord in his place. The means whereby you may swear allegiance to him is to bring him the head of your old Lord."

"I will not do this thing."

"I say that to do it willingly is the only means whereby you may keep your life within your body."

"I will not."

"You have said it. Now it is too late to save yourself. Still, you will do as I have ordered."

With this, a spirit not his own came into his body, and he found himself stooping, retrieving the blade. It burned his hands, but he raised it, held it and turned.

Cursing, weeping, he moved to the body, stood above it and brought the blade singing down. The head rolled several feet and blood darkened the stones.

"Now bring it to me."

He picked it up by the hair, held it at arm's length and returned to where he had stood. The other accepted it from him and swung it casually at his side.

"Thank you," he said. "Not a bad likeness at all." He hoisted it, studied it, swung it again. "No indeed. I wonder whatever became of my old one? No matter. I shall put this to good use."

"Kill me now," said Smage.

"I regret that I must save that chore for a bit later. For now, you may keep the remainder of your ex-Lord company here, by joining all but two others in sleep."

He gestured and Smage fell snoring to the ground; the flames died as he fell.

When the door opened, Evene did not turn to face it.

After a prolonged silence, she heard his voice and shuddered.

"You must have known," he said, "that eventually I would come for you."

She did not reply.

"You must recall the promise I made," he said.

She turned then, and he saw that she was weeping.

"So you've come to steal me?" she said.

"No," he said. "I came to make you the Lady of Shadow Guard—*my* Lady."

"To steal me," she repeated. "There is no other way you may have me now, and it is your favorite way of obtaining what you desire. You cannot steal love, though, Jack."

"That I can do without," he said.

"What now? To Shadow Guard?"

"Why, Shadow Guard is here. This place is Shadow Guard, nor am I ever out of it."

"I knew it," she said, very softly. ". . . And you mean to reign here, in his place, who is my Lord. *What have you done with him?*" she whispered.

"What did he do with me? What did I promise him?" he said.

". . And the others?"

"All are sleeping, save for one who may provide you some amusement. Let us step to the window."

Stiffly, she moved.

He swept the hanging aside and pointed. Inclining her head, she followed his gesture.

Below, on a level place which she knew had never before existed, Quazer moved. The gray, bisexual giant moved through the elaborate paces of the Helldance. He fell several times, rose to his feet, continued.

"What is he doing?" she asked.

"He is repeating the feat which won him the Hellflame. He will continue to reenact his triumph until his heart or some great vessel bursts within him and he dies."

"How awful! Stop him!"

"No. It is no more awful than what he had done to me. You accused me of not keeping my promises. Well, I promised him my vengeance, and you can see that I did not fail to deliver it."

"What power is it that you have?" she asked. "You could never do things like that when I— when I knew you."

"I hold The Key That Was Lost," he said, "Kolwynia."

"How did you come by it?"

"It does not matter. What does matter is that I can make the mountains walk and the ground burst open; I can call down bolts of lightning and summon spirits to aid me. I can destroy a Lord in his place of power. I have become the mightiest thing in the dark hemisphere."

"Yes," she said. "You have named yourself; you have become a thing."

He turned to watch Quazer fall again, then let the hanging drop.

She turned away.

"If you will grant mercy to all who remain here," she finally said, "I will do whatever you say."

With his free hand, he reached out as if to touch her. He paused when he heard the scream from beyond the window. Smiling, he let his hand fall. The taste is too sweet, he decided.

"Mercy, I have learned, is a thing that is withheld from one whenever he most needs it," he said. "Yet when he is in a position to grant it himself, those who withheld it previously cry out for it."

"I am certain," she said, "that no one in this place has asked mercy for himself."

She turned back to him and searched his face.

"No," she said. "No mercy there. Once there was something slightly gallant about you. It is gone now."

"What do you think I am going to do with the Key, after I have repaid my enemies?" he asked.

"I do not know."

"I am going to unite the darkside, making it into a single kingdom—"

"Ruled by yourself, of course."

"Of course, for there is no one else who

could do it. Then I am going to establish an era of law and peace."

"Your laws. Your peace."

"You still do not understand. I have thought of this for a long while, and while it is true that at first I sought the Key only for purposes of revenge, I have come to alter my thinking. I will use it to end the bickering of the Lords and promote the welfare of the state that will ensue."

"Then start here. Promote some welfare in High Dudgeon—or Shadow Guard, if you care to call it that."

"It is true that I have already repaid much that was done to me," he mused. "Still—"

"Begin with mercy and your name may one day be venerated," she said. "Withhold it and you will surely be cursed."

"Perhaps . . ." he began, taking a step backward.

Her eyes covered his entire form as he did so.

"What is it that you clutch beneath your cloak? You must have brought it to show me."

"It is nothing," he said. "I have changed my mind and there are things I must do. I will return to you later."

But she moved forward quickly and tore at his cloak as he turned.

Then the screams began, and he dropped

the head to seize her wrists. In her right hand there was a dagger.

"Beast!" she cried, biting his cheek.

He raised his will, uttered a single word, and the dagger became a dark flower which he forced toward her face. She spat and cursed and kicked him, but after a few moments her movements weakened and her eyelids began to droop. When she grew sufficiently drowsy, he carried her to her bed and placed her upon it. She continued to resist him, but the strength had gone out of her efforts.

"It is said that power can destroy all that is good in a man," she gasped. "But you need have no fear. Even without power, you would be what you are: Jack of Evil."

"So be it," he said. "Yet all that I have described to you will come to pass, and you will be with me to witness it."

"No. I will have taken my life long before."

"I will bend your will, and you will love me."

"You will never touch me, body or will."

"You will sleep now," he said, "and when you awaken we will be coupled. You will struggle briefly and you will yield to me—first your body, then your will. You will lie passive for a time, then I will come to you again and yet again. After that, it will be you who will come to me. Now you will sleep while I sacrifice Smage upon his Lord's altar and cleanse this place of all things which displease me. Dream well. A new life awaits you."

And he departed, and these things were done as he had said.

10

AFTER SOLVING ALL boundary problems involving Drekkheim by conquering that kingdom, adding it to his own, and sending the Baron to the Dung Pits, Jack turned his attention to the Fortress Holding, home of the Colonel Who Never Died. It was not long before the place betrayed its name, and Jack entered there.

He sat in the library with the Colonel and they sipped a light wine and reminisced for a long while.

Finally, Jack touched on the delicate subject of Evene's union with the suitor who obtained the Hellflame.

The Colonel, whose sallow cheeks bore matching crescent scars and whose hair funneled up from the bridge of his nose like a red tornado, nodded above his goblet. He dropped his pale eyes.

"Well, that was—the understanding," he said softly.

"It was not my understanding," said Jack. "I took it as a task you had set me to, not an offer open to all comers."

"You must admit that you did fail. So when another suitor appeared with the bride-price, I'd set—"

"You could have waited for my return. I would have stolen it and brought it to you."

"Return takes a goodly while. I did not want my daughter to become an old maid."

Jack shook his head.

"I confess that I am quite pleased with the way things have turned out," the Colonel continued. "You are a powerful Lord now, and you have my daughter. I would imagine she is happy. I have the Hellflame, and this pleases me. We all have what we wanted—"

"No," said Jack. "I might suggest that you never desired me for a son-in-law and that you obtained an understanding with the late Lord of High Dudgeon as to how the situation might best be settled."

"I—"

Jack raised his hand.

"I say only that I might suggest this. Of course, I do not. I do not really know what did or did not pass between you—other than Evene and the Hellflame—nor do I care. I know only what occurred. Considering this, and considering also the fact that you are now a relative, I shall allow you to take your own life, rather than lose it at the hands of another."

The Colonel sighed and smiled, raising his eyes once more.

"Thank you," he said. "That is very good of you. I was concerned that you might not give me this."

They sipped their wine.

"I shall have to change my appellation," said the Colonel.

"Not yet," said Jack.

"True, but have you any suggestions?"

"No. I shall meditate upon the question during your absence, however."

"Thank you," said the Colonel. "You know, I've never done anything like this before . . . Would you care to recommend any specific method?"

Jack was silent for a moment. "Poison is very good," he said. "But the effects vary so from individual to individual that it can sometimes prove painful. I'd say that your purposes would best be served by sitting in a warm bath and cutting your wrists under water. This hardly hurts at all. It is pretty much like going to sleep."

"I believe I'll do it that way then."

"In that case," said Jack, "let me give you a few pointers."

He reached forward, took the other's wrist and turned it, exposng the underside. He drew his dagger.

"Now then," he began, slipping back into a tutorial mode of speech he had all but forgotten, "do not make the same mistakes as most amateurs at this business." Using the blade as a pointer, he said, "Do not cut crosswise, so. Subsequent clotting might be sufficient to cause a reawakening, and the necessity to repeat the process. This could even occur several times. This would doubtless produce some trauma, as well as an aesthetic dissatisfaction. You must cut *lengthwise* along the blue line, here," he said, tracing. "Should the artery prove too slippery, you must lift it out with the point of your instrument and twist the blade quickly. Do not just pull upward. This is unpleasant. Remember that. The twist is the important part if you fail to get it with the lengthwise slash. Any questions?"

"I think not."

"Then repeat it back to me."

"Lend me your dagger."

"Here."

Jack listened, nodding, and made only minor corrections.

"Very good. I believe you've got it," he said, accepting the return of his blade and resheathing it.

"Would you care for another glass of wine?"

"Yes. You keep a fine cellar."

"Thank you."

High above the dark world, beneath the dark orb, mounted upon the lazy dragon to whom he had fed Benoni and Blite, Jack laughed into the winds and the fickle sylphs laughed with him, for he was their master now.

As time wore on, Jack continued to resolve boundary disputes to his satisfaction; and these grew fewer in number. He began, idly at first and then with growing enthusiasm, to employ the skills he had acquired dayside in the compilation of a massive volume called *An Assessment of Darkside Culture*. As his will now extended over much of the night, he began summoning to his court those citizens whose memories or special skills provided historical, technical or artistic information for his work. He was more than half-resolved to see it published dayside when completed. Now that he had established smuggling routes and acquired agents in major dayside cities, he knew that this could be accomplished.

He sat in High Dudgeon, now Shadow Guard, a great, sprawling place of high, torch-lit halls, underground labyrinths and many towers. There were things of great beauty there, and things of incalculable worth. Shadows danced in its corridors, and the facets of countless gems gleamed brighter than the sun of the one-half world. He sat in his library in Shadow Guard with its former

Lord's skull an ashtray on his desk, and he labored with his project.

He lit a cigarette (one of the reasons he had established a clandestine commerce), having found the dayside custom a pleasant thing, as well as a difficult habit to break. He was watching its smoke mingle with that of a candle and climb toward the ceiling, when Stab—a man-bat-man reconversion, who had become his personal servant—entered and halted at the prescribed distance.

"Lord?" he said.

"Yes?"

"There is an old crone at the gates who has asked to speak with you."

"I haven't sent for any old crones. Tell her to go away."

"She said that you had invited her."

He glanced at the small, black man, whose lengthy limbs and antenna-like plumes of white hair above an abnormally long face gave him a multi-tactic, insect-like appearance; he respected him, for he had once been an accomplished thief who had attempted to rob the former Lord of this place.

"Invitation? I recall no such thing. What was your impression of her?"

"She had the stink of the west upon her, sir."

"Strange . . ."

". . . And she requested that I tell you it's Rosie."

"Rosalie!" said Jack, lowering his feet from his desk and sitting upright. "Bring her to me, Stab!"

"Yes, sir," said Stab, backing away, as always, from any sudden display of emotions on his Lord's part.

Jack flicked an ash into the skull and regarded it.

"I wonder if you're coming around yet?" he mused. "I've a feeling you may be."

He scribbled a note, reminding himself to inflict several companies of men with severe head colds and set them to patrolling the Dung Pits.

He had emptied the skull and was straightening the papers on his desk when Stab escorted her into the room. Rising, he glanced at Stab, who departed quickly.

"Rosalie!" he said, moving toward her. "It is so good . . ."

She did not return his smile, but accepted the seat he offered, nodding.

Gods! She *does* look like a broken mop, he decided again, remembering. Still . . . It's Rosalie.

"So you have finally come to Shadow Guard," he said. "For that bread you gave me long ago, you shall always be well fed. For the advice you gave me, you will always be honored. You shall have servants to bathe you and dress you and wait upon you. If you wish to pursue the Art, I will instruct you in higher magics. Whatever you wish, you need but ask for it. We shall have a feast for you—as soon as it can be prepared! Welcome to Shadow Guard!"

"I did not really come to stay, Jack, just to look at you again—in your new gray garments and fine black cloak. And what shiny boots! You never used to keep them that way."

He smiled.

"I don't do as much walking as I once did."

". . . Or skulking about either. No need for that now," she said. "So you've got yourself a kingdom, Jack—the largest I know of. Are you happy with it?"

"Quite happy."

"So you went to the machine that thinks like a man, only faster. The one I warned you about. Isn't that so?"

"Yes."

". . . And it gave you The Key That Was Lost, Kolwynia."

He turned away, groped for a cigarette, lit it and inhaled. He looked at her then and nodded.

"But it is a thing I do not discuss," he said.

"Of course, of course," she said, nodding. "With it, though, you obtained power to match ambitions you once did not even know you possessed."

"I would say that you are correct."

"Tell me of the woman."

"What woman?"

"I passed a woman in the hall, a lovely thing,

dressed all in green to match her eyes. I said hello and her mouth smiled at me, but her spirit walked behind her weeping. What have you done to her, Jack?"

"I did what was necessary."

"You stole something from her—I know not what—as you have stolen from everyone you have known. Is there anyone you count as friend, Jack? Anyone from whom you have taken nothing but given something?"

"Yes," he replied. "He sits atop Mount Panicus, half of stone and half I know not what. Many times have I visited him and tried with all my powers to free him. Yet even the Key has proven insufficient."

"Morningstar . . ." she said. "Yes, it is fitting that your one friend should be the accursed of the gods."

"Rosie, why do you chastise me? I am offering to make up in any way that I can for what you have suffered on my account or any other."

"That woman I saw . . . Would you restore her to whatever she was before you stole from her—if that was what I most desired of you?"

"Perhaps," said Jack, "but I doubt you would ask it. Were I to do so, I feel that she would be hopelessly mad."

"Why?"

"Because of things she has seen and felt."

"Were you responsible for these things?"

"Yes, but she had them coming."

"No human soul deserves the suffering I saw walking behind her."

"Souls! Talk to me not of souls! Or of suffering either! Are you boasting that you have a soul and I do not? Or do you think I know nothing of suffering myself?—You are correct, though, in your observation concerning her. She is part human."

"But you have a soul, Jack. I brought it with me."

"I am afraid I do not understand . . ."

"You left yours behind in the Dung Pits of Glyve, as all darksiders do. I fetched yours out, though, in case you wanted it one day."

"You are joking, of course."

"No."

"Then how did you know it was mine?"

"I am a Wise Woman."

"Let me see it."

He mashed out his cigarette while she undid her parcel of belongings. She withdrew a small object wrapped in a piece of clean cloth. She opened the cloth and held it in the palm of her hand.

"That thing?" he said; and he began to laugh.

It was a gray sphere which began to brighten with exposure to the light, first becoming shiny and mirror-like, then translucent; colors began to shift across its surface.

"It's just a stone," he said.

"It was with you on your awakening in the Pits, was it not?"

"Yes. I had it in my hand."

"Why did you leave it behind?"

"Why not?"

"Was it not with you *each* time that you awakened in Glyve?"

"What of it?"

"It contains your soul. You may wish to be united with it one day."

"That's a soul? What am I supposed to do with it? Carry it around in my pocket?"

"You could do better than leave it on a pile of offal."

"Give it to me!"

He snatched it from her hand and stared at it.

"That's no soul," he said. "It is a singularly unattractive piece of rock, or perhaps the egg of a giant dung beetle. It even *smells* like the Pits!"

He drew his arm back to hurl it from him.

"Don't!" she cried. "It's your—soul . . ." she finished softly, as it struck against the stone wall and shattered.

Quickly, he turned his head away.

"I might have known," she said. "None of you really want them. You least of all. You must admit that there was something more to it than a simple stone or an egg or else you would not have acted with such instant rage. You sensed something personal and threatening about it. Didn't you?"

But he did not answer her. He had slowly turned his head in the direction of the broken thing and he was staring. She followed his gaze.

A misty cloud had emerged from the thing, spreading upward and outward. Now it hovered above it. It had ceased its movement and had begun to take color. As they watched, the outline of a man-like form began to appear.

Fascinated, Jack continued to stare as he saw that the deepening features were his own. It took on more and more of the appearance of solidity until it seemed that he regarded a twin.

"What spirit are you?" he inquired, his throat dry.

"Jack," it replied weakly.

"I am Jack," he said. "Who are you?"

"Jack," it repeated.

Turning to Rosalie, he snarled, "You brought it here! You banish it!"

"I cannot," she said, running a hand through her hair, then dropping it to her lap, where it joined the other and began a wringing motion. "It is yours."

"Why didn't you leave the damned thing where you found it? Where it belonged?"

"It didn't belong there," she said. "It is yours."

Turning back, he said, "You there! Are you a soul?"

"Wait a moment, will you?" it said. "I'm just putting things together.—Yes. Now that I think of it, I believe I am a soul."

"Whose?"

"Yours. Jack."

"Great," said Jack. "You've really paid me back, haven't you, Rosie? What the hell am I going to do with a soul? How do you get rid of one? If I die while this thing is loose, there is no return for me."

"I don't know what to tell you," she said. "I thought it was the right thing to do—when I went looking for it and found it—to bring it to you and give it to you."

"Why?"

"I told you long ago that the Baron was always kind to old Rosie. You hung him upside down and opened his belly when you took his realm. I cried, Jack. He was the only one who'd been kind to me for a long while. I'd heard much of your doings, and none of what I heard was good. With the power you have, it is so easy to hurt so many; and you have been doing it. I thought that if I went and found you a soul it might soften your disposition."

"Rosalie, Rosalie." He sighed. "You're a fool. You meant well, but you're a fool."

"Perhaps," she answered, squeezing her hands together tightly and looking back at the soul, which stood staring.

"Soul," said Jack, turning toward it again,

"you've been listening. Do you have any suggestions?"

"I have only one desire."

"What is that?"

"To be united with you. To go through life with you, comforting and cautioning, and—"

"Wait a moment," said Jack, raising his hand. "What does it require for you to be united with me?"

"Your consent."

Jack smiled. He lit a cigarette, his hands trembling slightly.

"What if I were to withhold my consent?" he asked.

"Then I would become a wanderer. I would follow you at a distance, unable to comfort you and caution you, unable—"

"Great," said Jack. "I withhold my consent. Get out of here."

"Are you joking? That's a hell of a way to treat a soul. Here I am, waiting to comfort and caution you, and you kick me out. What will people say? 'There goes Jack's soul,' they'll say, 'poor thing. Consorting with elementals and lower astrals and—'"

"Clear out," Jack said. "I can do without you. I know all about you sneaky bastards. You make people change. Well, I don't want to change. I'm happy the way I am. You're a mistake. Go back to the Dung Pits. Go wherever you want. Do whatever you want. Just go away. Leave me alone."

"You really mean it."

"That's right. I'll even get you a pretty new crystal, if you would prefer curling up inside one of those."

"It is too late for that."

"Well, that is the best I can offer."

"If you do not wish to be united with me, please do not throw me out like a vagabond. Let me stay here with you. Perhaps I can comfort and caution and counsel this way, and then you might see my value and change your mind."

"Get out!"

"What if I refuse to go? What if I simply force my attentions upon you?"

"Then," said Jack, "I would expose you to the most destructive powers of the Key, sections I've never essayed before."

"You would destroy your own soul?"

"You're damned right! Go away!"

It turned then toward the wall and vanished.

"So much for souls," said Jack. "Now we'll find you a chamber and some servants, and we'll see a feast prepared."

"No," she said. "I wanted to see you. Very well, I've seen you. I wanted to bring you a thing, and I've delivered it. That is all."

She began to rise.

"Wait," said Jack. "Where will you go?"

"My time as the Wise Woman of the Eastern

Marches having passed, I am returning to the
Sign of the Burning Pestle on the coach road by
the sea. Mayhap I will find some young tavern
wench to nurse me when I grow feeble. I'll teach
her of the Art in return for this."

"Stay awhile, at least," he said. "Rest, eat . . ."

"No. I do not like this place."

"If you are determined to go, allow me to
send you by an easier means than walking."

"No. Thank you."

"May I give you money?"

"I would be robbed of it."

"I will send an escort."

"I wish to travel alone."

"Very well, Rosalie."

He watched her depart and then moved to
the hearth, where he kindled a small fire.

Jack worked on his *Assessment*, becoming an
increasingly prominent figure in it, and he con-
solidated his rule of the night. During this time,
he saw countless statues of himself raised in the
land. He heard his name on the lips of ballad
singers and poets—not in the old rhymes and
songs of his roguery, but in tellings of his wisdom
and his might. On four occasions did he allow
the Lord of Bats, Smage, Quazer, the Baron and
Blite to return partway from Glyve, before he
sent them back again, each time in a different
fashion. He had decided to exhaust their alloted
lives and so be rid of them forever.

Evene danced and laughed at the feast Jack gave in honor of her father's return. Wrists still a-tingle, he raised in toast a wine from the cellar that had once been his.

"To the Lord and Lady of Shadow Guard," he said. "May their happiness and their reign endure as long as there is night to cover us!"

Then the Colonel Who Had Never Been Slain By Another quaffed it, and there was merriment.

High on Panicus, a part of Panicus, Morningstar regarded the east.

A soul wandered the night, cursing.

A fat dragon wheezed as he bore a sheep toward his distant den.

A beast in a twilit swamp dreamed of blood.

11

THEN CAME THE time of the true breaking of the Compact.

It grew cold, and he consulted the Book. He found the names of those whose turn had come. He waited and watched, but nothing occurred.

Finally, he summoned those dark Lords before him.

"Friends," he said, "it is yor turn for Shield duty. Why have you not done it?"

"Sir," said the Lord Eldridge, "we agreed to refuse it."

"Why?"

"You broke it yourself," he said. "If we cannot have the world the way that it was, we would like it to remain the way that it is. That is to say, on the pathway to destruction. Slay us if you wish, but we will not lift a hand. If you are such a mighty magician, repair the Shield yourself. Slay us, and watch the dying."

"You heard his request," Jack said to a servant. "See that they are slain."

"But sir—"

"Do as I say."

"Yes."

"I will attend to the Shield myself."

So they were taken and slain.

And Jack went forth.

On the top of a nearby mountain, he considered the problem. He felt the cold; he opened his being; he found the flaws in the Shield.

Then he began sketching the diagrams. With the point of his blade, he scratched them on a rock. They smoldered as he did so and then began to glow. He recited words from the Key.

"Uh—hello."

He whirled, raising the blade.

"It's just me."

He lowered it, and gusts of icy wind went by.

"What do you want, soul?"

"I was curious as to what you were doing. I sometimes follow you around, you know."

"I know. I don't like it."

He returned his attention to the diagram.

"Will you tell me?"

"All right," he said, "if it will keep you from whining around—"

"I'm a lost soul. We *do* whine."

"Then do it all you want. I don't care."

"But the thing you are doing . . ."

"I am about to repair the Shield. I think I have the spells worked out."

"I do not believe that you can."

"What do you mean?"

"I do not think it can be done by a single individual."

"Well, let's find out."

"May I help?"

"No!"

He returned to the pattern, elaborated upon it with his sword blade and continued his incantations. The winds went by and the fires flowed.

"Now I have to go," he said. "Stay out of my way, soul."

"All right. I just want to be united with you."

"Maybe sometime when life gets boring—but not now."

"You mean that there is hope?"

"Perhaps. Not at the present time, however."

Then Jack stood upright and regarded what he had done.

"Didn't work, did it?"

"Shut up."

"You failed."

"Shut up."

"Do you want to be united with me?"

"No!"

"Maybe I could have helped you."

"Try it in hell."

"Just asking."

"Leave me alone."

"What will you do now?"

"Go away!"

He raised his hands and hurled the power. It failed.

"I can't do it," he said.

"I knew that. Do you know what to do now?"

"I'm thinking."

"I know what to do."

"What?"

"Go check with your friend Morningstar. He knows lots of things. I believe he could advise you."

Jack lowered his head and stared at the smoldering pattern. The wind was chill.

"Perhaps you are right," he said.

"I feel certain that I am."

Jack swirled his cloak about him.

"I go now to walk in shadows," he said.

And Jack walked among shadows until he came to the place. Then he climbed.

When he reached the summit, he moved toward Morningstar and said, "I am here."

"I know."

"You also know what I desire?"

"Yes."

189

"Can it be accomplished?"

"It is not impossible."

"What must I do?"

"It will not be easy."

"I did not feel it would be. Tell me."

Morningstar shifted his great bulk slightly. And then he told him.

"I don't know that I can do it," Jack said.

"Someone must."

"Do you know of anyone else? Someone I might appoint?"

"No."

"Are you able to foretell my success or failure?"

"No. One other time I spoke of your shadows."

"Yes, I recall."

There was silence on the mountain. "Goodbye, Morningstar," Jack said. "Thank you."

"Farewell, Jack."

Turning, Jack moved into the shadows.

He entered the great hole that led to the heart of the world. In places, there were patches of light on the walls of the tunnel. Then he would enter into shadow and advance great distances in a brief time. In other places, the darkness was absolute and he went as others go.

Occasionally, there were strangely furnished side galleries and dark doorways. He did not pause to explore these. Infrequently, he heard the scurrying of clawed feet and the clatter of hooves. Once he passed an open hearth in which bones were burning. Twice he heard screams like those of a woman in pain. He did not pause, but loosened his blade in his scabbard.

He passed a gallery wherein a gigantic spider clung to the center of a rope-like web. It began to stir. He ran.

It did not pursue, but after a time he heard laughter far to his rear.

When he paused to refresh himself, he saw that the walls of that place were damp and mold-encrusted. He heard a sound like the flow of a distant river. Tiny crab-like creatures fled from him and clung to the walls.

Advancing farther, he encountered pits and crevasses from which noxious fumes arose; occasionally, flames leaped from one of these.

It was long before he came to the bridge of metal just a handspan in width. He looked into the abyss it crossed and saw only blackness. He poised himself, balanced carefully and passed slowly onward. He sighed when he set foot on the far side, and he did not turn and look back.

The walls of the tunnel widened and vanished now, and the ceiling rose into invisibility. Dark masses of varying density moved about him, and while he could at any time have created a small light to guide him, he feared to do so, because it could attract whatever was passing. A large light could be managed as well, but its existence would be brief; the moment he entered the world of the shadows it created it would cease to be, and he would stand in darkness once more.

For a time he feared he had entered a gigantic cavern and had gone astray there; but a ribbon of white appeared before him, and he held it with his eyes and continued to advance. When, after a long while, he came upon it, he saw that it was a large black pond with lights like fish scales glimmering upon it, cast from the faintly glowing fungus that covered the walls and roof of the cavern.

As he circled the pool, heading for a patch of great darkness beyond its opposite shore, there came a thrashing within the water. His blade was in his hand as he turned.

Having now been discovered, he spoke the words which caused an illumination to appear above the pool. A large ripple arrowed in his direction, as though a great bulk moved beneath it. From either of its sides now, a clawed tentacle rose, black and dripping, and extended itself in his direction.

He squinted against the light he had created and raised up his blade for a double-handed blow.

He spoke the quickest charm he knew to grant him strength and accuracy. Then, as soon as the nearest tentacle came within striking range, he swung and cut through it. It fell near his left boot, still writhing, struck against him and caused him to fall.

At this, he counted himself fortunate. For as he fell, the second tentacle slashed through the space his head and shoulders had occupied a moment before.

Then a round face, perhaps three feet in diameter, blank-eyed and crowned with a mass of writhing strands as thick as his thumb, exploded above the water, opened a large hole in its lower portion and moved toward Jack.

Not rising from where he lay, Jack swung the blade and pointed it directly at the thing, holding it with both hands, and he repeated words from the Key as rapidly as his mouth could form them.

His blade began to glow, there came a sputtering sound, then a stream of fire began to flow from the point of the weapon.

Jack moved the blade in a slow circle and the stench of burning flesh soon reached his nostrils.

Still, the creature continued to advance, until Jack saw the whiteness of its many teeth. Its good tentacle and the stub of its severed one flailed wildly, striking dangerously near. The beast gave a hissing, spitting sound. At that moment, Jack raised the blade, so that the fire fell upon the things that writhed on top of it.

With a sound that was almost like a sob, it threw itself backward into the pool.

Its bulk raised a wave that washed over Jack. But before it struck him and the beast vanished into the depths, he saw the creature's backside; and it was not the coldness of the water that caused him to shudder.

Rising then, he dipped his blade into the pool and repeated a spell to intensify a thousandfold the power he had called into the weapon. With this, the blade began to vibrate in his hands so that he could scarcely hold it. Yet he braced himself and stood there, the light blazing above and the stilled tentacle beside him.

The more he feared the power he had summoned, the longer it seemed that he stood there, and perspiration covered him like a sudden extra warm garment.

Then, with a hissing that was near to a shriek, half the creature's bulk rose with a rush of waters above the pool's center. As it vanished below once more, Jack did not move, but maintained his stance until the pool began to boil.

The creature did not rise again.

Jack did not eat until he had circled the pool and entered the far tunnel; and he knew that he dare not sleep. He strengthened himself with drugs and continued on.

Coming to a region of fires, he was attacked by a hairy man-beast and its mate. But he stepped into shadow, mocking them as they strove to reach him. Not wishing to waste time with torment and death, however, he renounced this pleasure and caused the shadows to transport him to their farthest limit.

The region of fires was vast, and a moment later when Jack stood at its far edge, he knew he was nearing his goal. There, he prepared himself for the next place of danger he must pass.

After a long walk, he began to detect the odors, reminding him of the Dung Pits of Glyve and something even more foul. He knew that soon he would be able to see again, though there would be no light and, consequently, no shadows into which he might escape. He rehearsed the necessary things.

The odors increased in intensity, until he fought with his stomach to retain what it held.

Then a gradual vision came into his eyes, unlike normal sight.

He saw a dank land of rocks and caverns, and all over it a certain mournful brooding lay. It was a still place, where mists twined slowly through the air and among the rocks, where faint vapors hung over large puddles of still water, where the odors and mists and vapors clotted together a brief distance overhead, to rain an occasional silent moment, redistributing the filth across the land. Beyond these things, there was nothing to be seen; and a bone-touching chill was everywhere.

He moved as quickly as he dared.

Before he had gone a great distance, he
detected the slightest of movements to his left.
He saw that in one of the normally still puddles
a tiny, dark creature covered with warty protu-
berances had hopped forth and now sat staring
at him, unblinking.

Drawing his blade, he touched it lightly with
its tip and took a rapid step backward, expecting
what might occur. The air exploded as the
creature was transformed. It towered above him
on crooked, black legs; it had no face, no apparent depth of body, but existed as if it were
drawn in outline with the darkest of inks. Those
were not feet it stood upon. Its tail twitched as
it spoke.

"Give me your name, that comes this way,"
said the voice that chimed like the silver bells of
Krelle.

"None may have my name ere I have his,"
said Jack.

A soft laughter emerged from the outline
of a horned head.

Then, "Come, come now! I wish to hear a
name," it said. "I have no patience."

"Very well, then," said Jack; and he spoke
one.

It fell to its knees before him.

"Master," it said.

"Yes," Jack replied. "That is my name. Now
must you obey me in all things."

"Yes."

"Now I charge you by that which I spoke, to bear me upon your back to the ultimate bounds of your realm, leading downward, until you are able to pass no farther, nor any others of your kind. Nor will you betray me to any of your kin or comrades."

"I will do as you have said."

"Yes."

"Repeat it back to me as an oath."

This was done.

"Bend now lower that I may mount you and you be my steed."

He leaped onto the creature's back, reached forth, caught hold of either horn.

"Now!" he said; and it rose and began to move.

There was a clatter of hooves and a bellows-like exhalation. He noted that the texture of the thing beneath him was not unlike that of a very soft cloth.

The pace quickened and the landscape began to blur whenever he attempted to fix his eyes.

. . . And then there was silence.

He became conscious of a black movement about him, and his face was fanned by breezes that came and went with the regularity of pulse-beats. He realized then that they were aloft, and that those were great black pinions that swept them above the noxious land.

They travelled for a long while, and Jack

wrinkled his nose, for the reek of the beast exceeded that of the countryside. They moved at a great speed, but he saw that similar dark shapes occasionally passed in the region of the upper air.

Despite their speed, the journey seemed interminable. Jack began to feel that his strength would fail, for his hands began to ache now even more than they had when he had boiled the black pool. He feared sleep, for his grip might fail him. So he thought upon many things to keep him awake. Strange, he thought, how my greatest enemy did me my greatest favor. Had the Lord of Bats not driven me to it, I would never have sought the power I now contain, the power that made me ruler, that gave me full revenge and Evene . . . Evene . . . I still am not fully pleased with the terms by which I hold you. Yet . . . What other way is there? You deserved what I did. Is not love itself a form of a spell, where one is loved and the other loves, and the one who loves is compelled to do the other's bidding? Of course. It is the same thing.

. . . And he thought then of the Colonel her father, and of Smage, Quazer, Blite, Benoni, the Baron. All of them paid now, all of them paid. He thought of Rosalie, old Rosie, and wondered whether she still lived. He resolved to inquire after her one day at the Sign of the Burning Pestle on the coach road by the ocean. The Borshin. He wondered whether the deformed creature had somehow survived, and still sought his trail somewhere, with but one burning imperative within his twisted body. He was truly the Lord of Bats' last weapon, his last hope for revenge. Like the explosion of a *geblinka* pod, this made his mind return to things he had not thought upon for a long while: the computers and The Dugout, the classes and that girl—what was her name?—Clare! He smiled that he remembered her name, although her face was but a blur now. And there was Quilian. He knew he would never forget Quilian's face. How he had hated the man! He chuckled at having left him in the hands of the pain-crazed Borshin, who had doubtless mistaken Quilian for himself. He remembered that mad drive across the country, fleeing the light, heading darkside, not knowing whether the print-outs he carried did indeed contain The Key That Was Lost, Kolwynia. The thought of his exultation when he tested it. Although he had never revisited the light, he now felt a strange nostalgia for those days at the university. Perhaps it is because I am outside now, he thought, and regarding this as an object; whereas then I was a part of the object itself.

. . . And always his thoughts returned to the towering figure of Morningstar atop Mount Panicus . . .

He reviewed his entire movement, from the Hellgames to his present situation, from the place where it had all started to this point in his current journey . . .

. . . And always his thoughts returned to Morningstar on Panicus, his only friend . . .

Why were they friends? What had they in common? Nothing that he could think of. Yet he felt an affection for the enigmatic being which he had never felt for another creature; and he felt that Morningstar, for some unknown reason, also cared for him.

. . . And it was Morningstar who had recommended this journey as the only means to accomplish what must be done . . .

Then he thought of the conditions which prevailed on the darkside of the world; and he realized that he, Jack, was not merely the only one capable of making the journey, but also was largely responsible for the state of affairs which required the journey. It was not, however, a sense of duty or responsibility that motivated him. Rather, it was one of self-preservation. If the darkside died in the freezing All-winter, he died with it; and there would be no resurrection.

. . . And always his thoughts returned to the towering figure of Morningstar on top of Mount Panicus . . .

The shudder that shook him then almost made him release the horns of the horrid creature he rode. The resemblance! The resemblance . . .

But no, he thought. This creature is but a

dwarf compared to Morningstar, who towers in the heavens. This thing hides its face, where Morningstar is nobly featured. This beast stinks, while Morningstar smells of the clean winds and rains of the heights. Morningstar is wise and kind, and this thing is stupid and wills but malice. It is but an accident that both are winged and horned. This creature may be bound by a magician's spell, and who could bind Morningstar . . . ?

Who indeed? he wondered. For is he not bound, though in a different fashion, as surely as I have bound this beast?—But it would take the gods themselves to do such a thing . . .

. . . And he pondered this and dismissed it.

It does not matter, he finally decided. He is my friend. I could ask this demon if he knows of him, but his reply would make no difference. Morningstar is my friend.

Then the world began to darken about him, and he tightened his grip for fear that he was growing faint. But as they swooped lower and the darkness deepened, he knew that they were nearing the edge of the realm.

Finally, the creature he rode alit. His sweet voice sang out:

"This far may I bear you, master, and no farther. That black stone before you marks the end of the realm of darkness visible. I may not pass it."

Jack passed beyond the black stone, and the blackness there was absolute.

Turning, he said, "Very well, then. I release you from my service, charging only that should we ever meet again, you will not attempt to harm me and shall serve my will as you have on this occasion. I bid you depart now. Go! You are sent forth!"

Then he moved away from that realm, knowing he was near to his goal.

He knew this because of the faint trembling of the ground beneath his feet. There was a barely perceptible vibration in the air, as of the hum of distant machinery.

He moved forward, meditating on his task. In a short while, magic would be ineffectual, the Key itself useless. But the black area through which he now proceeded should be empty of menace. It was simply the blackness that lay before the place. He caused a small light to occur intermittently, that his feet might be guided. He needed no guidance for direction; he had only to follow the sound and feel it strengthening.

. . . And as it strengthened, his ability to produce the guide light weakened and finally failed.

So he moved more carefully, not missing the tiny light too much because a pinpoint of light was now visible in the distance.

<u>12</u>

AS THE LIGHT grew in size, the humming and the vibrations increased in intensity. Finally, there was sufficient illumination for him to discern his course. After a time, the brightness was so intense that he cursed at having forgotten to bring his ancient sunglasses with him.

The brightness resolved itself into a square of light. He lay on his belly and looked at the light for a long period of time, allowing his eyes to make an adjustment. He repeated this many painful times as he advanced.

The floor of the place had become smooth beneath him; the air was cool but pleasant, and free of the odors which had prevailed in the region he had recently departed.

He moved until it was immediately before

him. There was nothing but the light. It was a gigantic opening onto something, but all that he could see was the yellow-white blaze; he heard a grinding, clanking and humming, as of many machines.

. . . Or the Great Machine.

Again, he lay prone. He crawled forward through the opening. He lay upon a ledge, and for a moment his mind could not assimilate all that was below.

It had so many gears that it would have been an interminable task to number them, some turning slowly, some rapidly, big unto small; and there were cams, drive shafts, and pulleys and pendulums—some of the pendulums twenty times his own height and slow, ponderous—and pistons and things that corkscrewed in and out of black metal sockets; and there were condensers, transformers and rectifiers; there were great blue-metal banks containing dials, switches, buttons and little lights of many colors, which constantly blinked on and off; there was the steady noise, a hum, of still further buried generators— or perhaps they were something else, possibly drawing power from the planet itself, its heat, its gravitational field, certain hidden stresses— which buzzed in his ears like a swarm of insects; there was the blue smell of ozone, reaching everywhere. There was the brilliant light coming from all the walls of the enormous cavern which housed the equipment; there was a battery of buckets which moved on guidelines above the entire complex, occasionally pausing in their courses to dump lubricants at various points; there were power cables, like snakes, that wound from one point to another, indicating nothing he could understand; there were tiny, glass-enclosed boxes, connected with the whole by means of thin wires, which contained components so minute that he could not discern their forms from where he lay. There were no fewer than a hundred elevator-type mechanisms, which constantly plunged into the depths or vanished overhead, and which paused at various levels of the machine to extrude mechanical appurtenances into portions of its mechanism; there were wide red bands of light on the farthest wall, and they flicked on and off; and his mind could not encompass all that he saw, felt, smelled and heard—though he knew that he must deal with it somehow—so that he searched for a clue for the best point of impact, seeking within that massive structure for that which would destroy it. He found titanic tools hung upon the walls, tools which could only have been wielded by giants, to service the thing—wrenches, pliers, pry bars, things-that-turned-other-things—and he knew that among them lay the thing that he required, a thing which, if properly employed, could break the Great Machine.

He crept farther forward and continued to stare. It was magnificent; there had never been anything like it before, and there never would be again.

He looked for a way down and saw a metal ladder, far off to his right. He went toward it.

The ledge narrowed, but he managed to reach the topmost rung, and from there he swung himself into position.

He began the long climb down.

Before he had reached the bottom, he heard footsteps. They were barely discernible over the sounds of the machinery, but he distinguished them and backed into a shadow.

Although the shadow did not possess its normal effects, it hid him. He waited there, near to the ladder, next to a generator of sorts, and thought of his next move.

A small, white-haired man limped by. Jack studied him. The man paused, found an oilcan, dripped lubricant upon various of the gears.

Jack watched as the man moved about the Machine, finding various slots and openings, squirting oil into them.

"Hello," he said, as the man passed.

"What—Who are you?"

"I am one who has come to see you."

"Why?"

"I came to ask you some questions."

"Well, that is pleasant enough and I am willing to answer you. What do you wish to know?"

"I was curious about the makeup of this Machine."

"It's quite complex," he replied.

"I daresay. Could you give me details?"

"Yes," he answered, dazzling him with the explanation.

Jack nodded his head and felt his hands grow stiff.

"You understand?"

"Yes."

"What is the matter?"

"I believe that you are going to die," he said.

"What—" And Jack hit him in the left temple with the first knuckle of his right hand.

Crossing to a rack of tools near the Machine, he studied the great array of equipment. He selected a heavy bar of metal, whose function he did not understand. Lifting it, he sought a small glass case the old man had indicated. He studied the hundreds of tiny, delicate gears which turned within it, moving at varying rates of speed.

Raising the bar, he smashed the glass, and began to destroy the intricate mechanism. With each blow he struck, a sound of mechanical protest arose from some new portion of the vast Machine. There came an irregular humming, then a series of clanking sounds, as if something large had snapped or been torn loose. This was followed by a shrill whine, a grating sound and the screech of metal against metal. Then came a banging noise, and smoke began to rise from several segments. One of the more massive gears slowed, hesitated, halted, and began again, moving more slowly than before.

While Jack was smashing the other cases, the lubricant buckets went wild overhead, racing back and forth, emptying their contents, returning to the wall spigots for more. There came the smell of burning insulation and a popping, sizzling sound. The floor began to shake and several pistons tore loose. Now there were flames amid the smoke, and Jack coughed at the acrid fumes.

The Machine quivered, ground to a halt, and began again, wildly. It shook as gears raced and axles snapped. It began tearing itself to pieces. The din grew painful to his ears. Wheeling, he hurled the bar into the Machine and fled in the direction of the ladder.

When he looked back, there were huge figures, partly hidden by the smoke, racing toward the Machine. Too late, he knew.

He fled up the ladder, reached the ledge, raced into the darkness from which he had come.

Thus began the destruction of the world he had known.

The return journey proved in some ways more dangerous than the downward one had been, for the ground trembled now, stirring the dust and debris of the ages, cracking walls, causing portions of the roof to collapse. Twice, coughing, he had to clear litter from his way before he could pass. Then, too, the inhabitants of that great tunnel ran in panic, attacking one another with a new ferocity. Jack slew many to pass there.

After emerging, he looked at the black orb, high in the heavens. The coldness still came by it, more perhaps now than when he had begun his mission of sabotage. He studied that sphere and saw that it appeared to have moved slightly from the position it had previously occupied.

Then, hurriedly, to keep a recent promise he had made to himself, he employed the Key to transport him to the Sign of the Burning Pestle, on the coach road by the ocean.

He entered that inn, built of nightwood, repaired a thousand times, and ancient almost beyond his memory. As he descended into the central dining area, the ground shuddered and the walls creaked about him. This caused a silence, followed by a babble of voices, from a group of diners near the fire.

Jack approached them.

"I'm looking for an old woman named Rosalie," he said. "Does she reside here?"

A broad-shouldered man with a blond beard and a livid scar on his forehead, looked up from his meal.

"Who are you?" he asked.

"Jack of Shadow Guard."

The man studied his clothing, his face; his eyes widened, then dropped.

"I know of no Rosalie, sir," he said in a soft tone. "Do any of you others?"

The other five diners said, "No," keeping their eyes averted from Jack, and hastily added, "sir," to this reply.

"Who is the proprietor here?"

"Haric is his name, sir."

"Where may I find him?"

"Through that far doorway to your right, sir."

Jack turned and walked toward it. As he went, he heard his name whispered in shadows.

He mounted two stairs and entered a smaller room, where a fat, red-faced man, wearing a dirty apron, sat drinking wine. A yellow candle, sputtering on the table before him, made his face seem even ruddier. His head turned slowly, and it took his eyes several moments to focus as he peered in Jack's direction.

Then, "What do you want?" he asked.

"My name is Jack, and I've traveled far to reach this place, Haric," he replied. "I seek an old woman who was coming here to spend her final days. Her name is Rosalie. Tell me what you know of her."

Haric creased his brow, lowered his head and squinted.

"Bide a moment," he said. "There *was* an old hag . . . Yes. She died some time ago."

"Oh," said Jack. "Tell me then where she is buried, that I might visit her grave."

Haric snorted and quaffed his wine. Then he began to laugh. He wiped his mouth on the back of his hand, then raised it to wipe his eyes with his sleeve.

"Buried?" he said. "She was worthless. We only kept her here for charity's sake, and because she knew somewhat of healing."

Tiny bulges of muscle appeared at the hinges of Jack's jaws.

"Then what did you do with her?" he inquired.

"Why we threw her carcass into the ocean.— Small pickings there for fishes, though."

Jack left the Sign of the Burning Pestle burning at his back, there on the coach road by the ocean.

Beside the flat, black ocean, he now walked. The stars within it danced whenever the ground and the waters trembled. The air was quite chill, and he felt a great fatigue. His sword belt was almost too heavy to bear. He longed to wrap his cloak about him and lie down for a moment. He wanted a cigarette.

As he advanced like a sleepwalker, his boots sinking into the sand, he was shocked back to wakefulness at the sight of the one who appeared before him.

It appeared to be himself.

He shook his head, then, "Oh, it's you, soul," he said.

His soul nodded.

"There was no need for you to destroy that inn," it said, "for soon the seas will be unchained and mighty waves will wash the land. It would have been one of the first things destroyed."

"You are incorrect," said Jack, yawning. "There was reason: it did my heart good.—How is it that you know of the seas' coming behavior?"

"I am never far from you. I was with you atop Mount Panicus, when you spoke with mighty Morningstar. I descended with you into the bowels of the world. When you smashed the Great Machine, I stood at your side. I returned with you. I accompanied you to this place."

"Why?"

"You know what it is that I want."

". . . And you have had my answer on numerous occasions."

"You know that this time it is different, Jack. By your actions, you are stripping yourself of most of your powers—perhaps all of them. You have possibly destroyed all your lives, save for the present one. You need me now. You know that you do."

Jack stared at the ocean and the stars darting like luminous insects.

"Possibly," he said. "But not yet."

"Look to the east, Jack. Look to the east."

Jack raised his eyes, turned his head.

"That is the inn, burning," he said.

"Then you will not see us united?"

212

"Not now. But neither will I drive you away. Let us return now to Shadow Guard."

"Very well."

Then the ground shook with its most terrific tremor thus far, and Jack swayed where he stood.

When the land grew still once again, he drew his blade and began to trace a pattern in the sand.

He began to pronounce the spell. As he was nearing its completion, he was dashed from his feet by a great wave which covered him over completely. He felt himself flung upon higher ground, and his lungs burned for air. He tried to follow it even farther, knowing what would happen next.

Lights darted before his eyes as he dug at the sand and pushed forward. He made some progress in this fashion before the waters began to recede.

He fought their pull, clawing at the sand, making sculling motions with his hands, kicking out with his feet, trying to crawl . . .

. . . And then he was free.

He lay with half his face in the cold, wet grit, his fingernails broken, his boots filled with water.

"Jack! This way! Hurry!"

It was his soul calling.

He lay there, gasping, unable to move.

"You must come, Jack! Or accept me now! There will be another wave shortly!"

Jack groaned. He tried to rise, failed.

Then from the inn, whose flames cast a pale, ruddy glow along the beach, there came a crash as the roof and one wall collapsed.

There was some blockage of the light now, and shadows danced about him.

Almost weeping, he drew strength from them each time they fell upon him.

"You must hurry, Jack! It's turned! It's coming!"

He rose to his knees, then pushed himself to his feet. He staggered forward.

He reached higher ground and continued inland. He saw his soul waiting up ahead and moved toward it.

Behind him, there came the rising sound of the waters now.

He did not look back.

Finally, he heard the wave break and he felt the spray. Only the spray.

He grinned weakly at his soul.

"You see? I did not require your services, after all," he said.

"You will soon, though," said his soul, smiling back.

Jack felt at his belt for his dagger, but the ocean had taken it from him, along with his cloak. His sword, which had been in his hand when the wave struck, had gone the same way.

"So the sea has robbed the thief." He chuckled. "It makes things more difficult."

He dropped to his knees and, wincing because of the broken nail, retraced the pattern he had drawn on the beach, using his forefinger.

Then, without rising, he spoke the spell.

He knelt in his great hall in Shadow Guard, and torches and enormous tapers flickered all about. For a long while, he did not move, and let the shadows bathe him. Then he stood and leaned against the wall.

"What now?" his soul asked him. "Will you cleanse yourself and sleep a long while?"

Jack moved his head.

"No," he replied. "I would not risk missing the time of my greatest triumph—or failure, as the case may be. I will bide here a moment, then fetch strong drugs to keep me alert, to give me strength."

He then moved to the cabinet where he kept his drugs, unlocked it by uttering the spell of the door, and prepared himself a draft. As he did so, he noticed that his hands shook. Before drinking the orange liquid, he had to spit several times to clear his mouth of sand.

Then he closed the cabinet and proceeded to the nearest bench.

"You have not slept in a long while—and you took similar drugs on your way to the Great Machine."

"I believe I am even more aware of this than you," said Jack.

"The strain on you will be considerable."

Jack did not reply. After a time, there came a tremor. Still, he said nothing.

"It's taking longer to affect you this time, isn't it?"

"Shut up!" said Jack.

Then he rose to his feet and raised his voice.

"Stab! Damn it! Where are you? I've come home!"

After a brief while, the dark one entered, almost scurrying.

"Lord! You've returned! We did not know . . ."

"Now you do. Bring me a bath, fresh clothing, a new blade and food—lots of it! I'm starving! Shake your ass!"

"Yes, sir!"

And Stab was gone.

"Do you feel insecure, that you need a blade about you in your own redoubt, Jack?"

He turned and smiled.

"These are special times, soul. If you've stayed as near to me as you say you have, you know that I did not ordinarily go in such fashion within these walls. Why do you seek to irritate me?"

"It is a soul's privilege—you might even say, duty—to occasionally do so."

"Then find a better time to exercise your privilege."

"But now is the perfect time. Jack—the most

appropriate which has occurred so far. Do you fear that if you lose your powers your subjects may rise up against you?"

"Shut up!"

"You know, of course, that they call you Jack of Evil."

Jack smiled once again.

"No," he said. "It will not work. I will not allow you to anger me, to trick me into something foolish.—Yes, I am aware of the title they have given me, although few have ever said it to my face, and none of these a second time. Do you not realize, however, that were any one of my subjects to occupy my position, he would soon come to bear a similar title?"

"Yes, I do realize this. It is because they lack souls."

"I will not argue with you," said Jack. "Though I would like to know why it is no one ever comments on your presence?"

"I am only visible to you, and then only when I wish to be."

"Excellent!" said Jack. "Why don't you become invisible to me now, too, and leave me to my bath and my meal?"

"Sorry. I am not quite ready."

Jack shrugged and turned his back.

After a time, his tub was brought in and filled with water. Some of it was spilled by a world shudder so violent that it sent a jagged crack like black lightning across one wall. Two candles toppled and were broken. A ceiling stone fell in a nearby chamber, harming no one.

Before he had fully undressed, a fresh blade was brought to him. He paused to test it, then nodded.

Before he had entered the tub, fresh garments were laid beside him on a bench.

Before he had finished bathing, a table was set nearby.

By the time he had dried himself, dressed and picked up his blade, the food was upon the table and his place was set.

He ate slowly, savoring each mouthful. He ate an enormous quantity.

Then he rose and retired to his study, where he located cigarettes. From there he moved to the foot of his favorite tower and mounted its stair.

Atop this tower, smoking, he studied the black sphere. Yes, it had moved considerably since last he had looked at it. Jack blew smoke in its direction. Perhaps it was an effect of the drugs, but he felt a sense of elation over what he had done. Come what comes, he was the mover, father of the new circumstances.

"Are you sorry now, Jack?" asked his soul.

"No," said Jack. "It had to be done."

"But are you *sorry* it had to be done?"

"No," said Jack.

"Why did you burn the inn at the Sign of

the Burning Pestle, on the coach road by the ocean?"

"To avenge Rosalie, for the treatment she received at that place."

"What were your feelings as you walked along the beach afterward?"

"I don't know."

"Were you just angry and tired? Or was it more than that?"

"I was sad. I was sorry."

"Do you get that way very often?"

"No."

"Do you wish to know why you have felt more such things recently?"

"If you know, tell me."

"It is because I am about. You have a soul, a soul which has been freed. I am always near you. You have begun to feel my influence. Is it such a bad thing?"

"Ask me another time," said Jack. "I came to watch things, not to talk."

. . . And his words reached the ears of one who sought him, as a distant mountain shrugged off its peak, spewed fire into the air, belched and was still once again.

13

JACK LISTENED TO the sound of snapping rocks and watched the black spot fall; he heard the groans within the world; he saw the lines of fire cross the land.

There now came to his nostrils the acrid odors of the inner world. Ashes, like the bats of his predecessor, swarmed, rose, fell in the chilly air. The stars executed movements never before recorded in the heavens. Seven torch-topped mountains stood in the distance, and he recalled the day he had made one move. Flocks of meteors constantly strung the sky, reminding him of the appearance of the heavens on the day of his last resurrection. Clouds of vapor and trails of smoke occasionally obscured the constellations. The ground did not cease its trembling, and far below him Shadow Guard was shaken upon its foundation. He did not fear the falling of the tower, for such was his fondness of the place that he had laid mighty spells upon it and knew that it would stand so long as his power held.

His soul stood silent at his side. He lit another cigarette and watched a landslide on a nearby mountain.

Slowly the clouds gathered. They collected in the distance, where a storm began. Like many-legged, fiery-legged insects, they strode from mountain to mountain. They lit up the northern sky, were assailed by the meteorites, were spat at by the attacked land. After a time, Jack could hear the growling attendant upon the conflict. After a greater time, he noted that the battle was moving in his direction.

When it was almost upon him, Jack smiled and drew his blade.

"Now, soul," he said, "we'll see how my powers hold."

With this, he scratched a pattern on the stone and spoke.

The river of light and thunder parted, flowing about Shadow Guard, passing it on either side, leaving it untouched.

"Very good."

"Thank you."

They now stood enveloped: the ground burned and shook beneath them, the storm

221

raged about them, the sky was barred by shooting stars above.

"Now how will you be able to tell?"

"I'll be able to tell. In fact, a lot can be told already, can it not?" Jack said.

His soul did not reply.

Hearing a footfall, he turned toward the stair.

"It will be Evene," he said. "Storms frighten her, and she always comes to me when they occur."

Evene emerged from the stairwell, saw Jack, rushed to his side. She did not speak. He wrapped his cloak and his arm about her. She stood there shivering.

"Do you not feel any remorse over what you have done to her?"

"Some," said Jack.

"Then why do you not undo it?"

"No."

"Is it that remembering, she would hate you?"

Jack did not reply.

"She cannot hear me. If I phrase questions, you could reply briefly and she would think you are but muttering.—Is it more than hate?"

"Yes."

Both were silent for a time. "Is it that you fear she will go mad if restored?"

"Yes."

"This means you possess more emotions and

sentiments than once you did, more than I had even suspected."

Jack did not reply.

The noise and the flashing lights were still all about them, and Evene finally turned her head, faced him and said, "It is terrible up here. Shall we go below, my dear?"

"No. You may, if you wish. But I must remain."

"Then I will stay with you."

Slowly, very slowly, the storm began to pass, died down, was gone. Jack saw that the mountains still burned, saw too, that the ruptured land heaved forth fires of its own. Turning, he noted a whiteness in the air that he finally realized was not smoke, but snow. This was far to the west, however.

He had a sudden feeling that it was not going to work, that the devastation would be too complete. But there was nothing to do now but watch.

"Evene . . . ?"

"Yes, Lord?"

"I have a thing to say . . ."

"What is it, my love?"

"I—Nothing!"

And his soul drew nearer, standing directly behind him now, and the strange feeling rose until he could bear it no longer.

Turning back to her, he said, "I am sorry!"

"For what, my dear?"

"I cannot explain it now, but there may come a time when you recall that I said it."

Puzzled, she said, "I hope that such a time never comes, Jack. I have always been happy with you."

He turned away and his eyes went to the east. He stopped breathing for a moment and he felt his heartbeat everywhere in his body.

Through the dust, the noise, the chill, it followed the trail. The flaring lights, the trembling land, the stalking storm meant nothing to it, for it had never known fear. It glided down hills like a ghost and slithered among rocks like a reptile. It leaped chasms, dodged falling stones, was singed once by lightning. It was a blob of protoplasm on a stick; it was a scarred hulk, and there was no real reason why it should be living and moving about. But perhaps it did not truly live—at least, not as other creatures, even darkside creatures, lived. It had no name, only an appellation. Its mentality, presumably, was not great. It was a bundle of instincts and reflexes, some of them innate. It was lacking in emotions, save for one. It was incredibly strong, and capable of enduring extreme privation, great amounts of pain and excessive bodily damage. It spoke no language, and all creatures it encountered fled from it.

While the ground shook and the rocks rattled about it, it began its descent of the mountain-which-once-had-moved, currents of blazing cloud dropping fires along its way.

The landslide did not stop it any more than the tempest could.

It picked its way among the strewn boulders at the mountain's base and for a moment regarded the final ascent.

There led the trail; there must it follow.

High, high-set, walled and well guarded . . .

But in addition to its strength it possessed a certain cunning.

. . . And its one emotion.

"Win or lose, it's working," Jack said; and although Evene did not reply, his soul did.

"You lose. Whether it is the world's gain or loss is another matter. But *you* lose, Jack."

. . . And as he gazed into the lightening east, Jack felt that this was true.

For the sky had grown pale of something other than volcanic fires and storms. Within him, he felt his power begin to break. Turning to the west, he saw again how far the black orb had fallen, and the dawn exploded in his mind.

As his power slipped away, the walls of Shadow Guard began to crumble.

"We'd best flee now."

"What do you care, spirit? You can't be harmed. I'll not flee. I say this tower will stand against the dawn."

Below him, stones and masonry raining into

a courtyard, a wall gave way, revealing the interiors of several chambers. Jack heard the cries of his servitors and several rushed across the courtyard. There came another shaking of the ground and the tower itself swayed slightly.

Jack faced the pink-skied east once more. "The Key That Was Lost, Kolwynia, is lost again," he said. "This time forever."

For he had tried a simple spell and it had failed.

He heard a roaring, as of waters unlocked, and a far portion of the citadel burst and was scattered.

"If you will not flee, then what of the girl who stands by your side?"

Jack turned toward Evene, having almost forgotten her presence. He saw that a curious look had come onto her face.

At first, he was unable to fathom her expression; and when she spoke, he noted that the timbre of her voice had changed.

"What is happening, Jack?"

As she spoke, he felt her body stiffen and sway slightly away from him. He immediately relaxed his arm to accommodate her movement.

In an instant, it filled his mind. With the slipping away of his magical powers, the spell he had laid upon her so long ago was coming undone. As the dawn spread over the troubled world, her mind cleared proportionately.

He began to speak, hoping to occupy her

full attention, to keep her from suddenly considering her changing condition.

"It is my doing," he stated. "The seven listed in the Red Book of Ells would not cooperate in maintaining the Shield against the outer cold, so I slew them. I was mistaken, however, in considering them expendable. Though I had thought I could manage it, I proved incapable of performing the feat on my own. There was but one alternative. I destroyed the Great Machine which maintained the world as it was. Now, we darksiders, drawing our legends from that near-incomprehensible thing called science, say it is a Machine that drives the world. The daysiders, equally superstitious, see the world's core as filled with fire elementals and molten minerals. Who is to say who is correct and who, incorrect? Philosophers on both sides have often speculated that the world of the senses is an illusion. It does not really matter to me. Whatever the reality from which we appear to be permanently isolated, I journeyed to the world's center and effected a catastrophe there. You see its results all about you now. Because of my actions, the world is beginning to rotate. There will no longer be a darkside and a lightside. Rather, there will be both darkness and light in succession in all portions of the world. The darkness, I feel, will always hold in some form the things we have held, and science will doubtless prevail in the light."

That is, he added mentally, if the world is not destroyed.

He wondered, at that moment, what it was like in the lands of light—back at the university—to have evening come on, then darkness, to see the stars. Would Poindexter think it an elaborate semester's end prank?

"This way," he went on, "there will be no need to shield against the cold or the heat. The warmth of the star about which we move will be distributed rather than concentrated. I—"

"Jack of Evil!" she cried, backing quickly away from him.

From the corner of his eye, he saw that a blazing orange arc had appeared above the horizon.

As its rays fell upon them, the tower trembled, quaked, began to rock violently. He heard the sound of falling stones within the tower itself, felt through his boots the vibrations of their dislodgment.

. . . And Evene crouched, and her eyes were wide and wild behind the masses of her now freed hair, which the wind whipped past them . . .

. . . And he saw that in her right hand she held a dagger.

He licked his lips and backed away.

"Evene," he said. "Please listen to me. I can take that toy away from you, but I don't want to hurt you. I've hurt you enough. Put it away, please. I'll try to make—"

She sprang at him then, and he reached for her wrist, missed, stepped to the side.

The blade went by; her arms and shoulder followed. He seized her shoulders.

"Jack of Evil!" she said again; and she slashed at his hand, cutting it.

As his grip weakened, she broke free and was upon him, thrusting for his throat.

He blocked her wrist with his left forearm and pushed her away with his right hand. He glimpsed her face as he did so, and there were flecks of foam at the corners of her mouth; lines of blood crossed her chin from where she had bitten her lip.

She stumbled back against the balustrade and it gave way, almost soundlessly.

He lunged toward her, but arrived only in time to see her billowing skirts as she fell toward the courtyard below. Her scream was brief.

He drew back when the tower's shifting threatened to topple him, also.

The sun was now half-risen.

"Jack! You've got to leave! The place is falling apart!"

"It doesn't matter," he said.

But he turned and headed toward the stair-well.

It searched the corridors, after having entered the citadel through a gaping hole in its northern wall. It left the bodies where they fell, whenever it had to slay. At one point, a section of roofing fell upon it. It dug its way out and continued on.

It crouched behind rubble as brigades of water-bearers rushed by to quench flames; it concealed itself in niches, and behind hangings, furniture, doors; it glided like a ghost and slithered like a reptile.

It picked its way through the debris until it located the trail once more.

High, high it led, and winding . . .

There would it go.

The sky split by the light, the broken balustrade so clear in his mind, the flower of her skirts blooming behind his eyes, her spittle and blood the ink of his indictment, the thunder of the tortured land a form of silence by virtue of its monotony, the shattered stones sharpened by dawn's shadowy clarity, the winds a dirge, the movements of the decaying tower an almost soothing thing now, Jack came to the head of the stairwell and saw it ascending.

He drew his blade and waited, as there was no other way down.

Strange, he thought, how the instinct to survive prevails, no matter what.

He held the point of his blade steady as the Borshin sprang up the final steps and attacked.

It pierced the creature's left shoulder, but

did not halt it. The blade was torn from his grasp, as the Borshin struck him, knocked him over backward, leaped for him.

He rolled to the side and managed to achieve a crouched position before the creature attacked him again. His blade was still in its shoulder, gleaming in the light; no blood lay upon it, but a thick, brownish fluid was oozing slightly about the edges of the wound.

He managed to dodge the second onslaught and strike it with both hands, but the blows had no apparent effect. It felt as if he were striking a pudding that would not splatter.

Twice more, he succeeded in evading its attack, kicking its leg once in the process and jabbing the back of its head with his elbow as it passed.

Next, it caught him loosely, but he jostled the blade within its shoulder and escaped with a torn tunic.

Crouching, circling, attempting to keep as much distance as possible between them, he scooped up two pieces of masonry and leaped backward. It would have had him then, save for his leap. It turned with great speed, and he hurled one of his new found weapons, missing.

Then, before he could recover from his throwing stance, it was upon him, bearing him over backward.

He struck it about the head with his remaining weapon, until it was dashed from his hand. His chest was being crushed, and the creature's face was so near his own that he wanted to scream, would have screamed, had he the breath.

"It is unfortunate that you did not choose properly," he heard his soul saying.

Then the creature's one hand came to the back of his neck and the other to his head. They began a twisting motion.

As the blackness rose from his middle and the tears of pain mingled with the perspiration on his face, his head was turned in such a fashion that he saw a thing which gave him an instant's wonder.

The magic was fled, but this dawn was still like twilight. He had been able to function in Twilight, not as a magician, but as a thief.

Because of his power within shadow.

. . . No blade could touch him there, no power harm him.

The rising sun, striking a section of balustrade, cast a long dark shadow that fell but a foot away.

He struggled to reach it, but could not. So he flung his right arm as far in that direction as it would go.

His hand and half his forearm fell within the shadow.

The pain was still there, and the creaking of vertebrae; he still felt the crushing weight upon his chest.

Only now, the old, dark feeling entered him and flowed through his body.

He resisted unconsciousness; he stiffened his neck muscles. With the strength he had drawn, he twisted and pushed until he had dragged his entire arm and shoulder into the shadow. Then, using his elbows and heels, he managed to force his head within the potent shade.

He pulled his other arm free and his hands found the Borshin's throat. He dragged him into the shadow with him.

"Jack, what is happening?" he heard his soul say. "I cannot see you when you are in shadow."

After a long while, Jack emerged from the shadow.

He leaned heavily upon the nearest balustrade and stood there panting. He was smeared with blood and a gummy, brownish substance.

"Jack?"

His hand shook as he reached within what remained of his tunic.

"Damn . . ." he half-whispered, hoarsely. "My last cigarettes are crushed."

He seemed as if he were about to cry over the fact.

"Jack, I did not think you would survive—"

"Neither did I.—All right, soul. You've bothered me long enough. I've been through much. There is nothing left for me. I may as well make you happy, anyhow. I give you my consent. Do what you would."

Then he closed his eyes for a moment, and when he opened them, his soul had vanished.

"Soul?" he inquired.

There was no reply.

He felt no different. Were they truly united?

"Soul? I gave you what you wanted. The least you can do is talk to me."

No answer.

"All right! Who needs you?"

Then he turned and looked out over the devastated land. He saw how the slanting rays of the sun brought color to the wilderness he had wrought. The winds had subsided somewhat, and it was as if there were a singing in the air. For all the wreckage and smoldering, there was a blasted beauty to the place. It would not have been necessary that it be racked so, had it not been for that within him which had brought pain, death and dishonor where it had not been before. Yet, out of the carnage, or rather, overlaying it now, was something he had never seen previously. It was as if everything he looked at contained the possibility of perfection. There were smashed villages in the distance, truncated mountains, charred forests. All the evil was upon his head, for he had indeed earned the title he had borne. Yet, out of it, he felt, some other thing would grow. For this, he could take no credit. He could only bear blame. But he felt that he was no longer precluded from seeing what might come now that the order of the world had been altered, from feeling it, delighting in it, perhaps even—No, not that. Not yet, anyhow. But the succession of light and darkness would be a new order of things, and he felt that this would be good. He turned then and faced the sunrise, wiped his eyes and stared some more, for he felt it the most lovely thing he had ever seen. Yes, he must have a soul, he decided, for he had never felt this way before.

The tower ceased its swaying and began to come apart about him.

I meant it, Evene, he thought. I even said it back before I had a soul. I said I was sorry and I meant it. Not just for you. For the whole world. I apologize. I love you.

. . . And stone by stone, it collapsed; and he was pitched forward toward the balustrade.

It is only fitting, he thought, as he felt himself strike the rail. It is only fitting. There is no escape. When the world is purged by winds and fires and waters, and the evil things are destroyed or washed away, it is only fitting that the last and greatest of them all be not omitted.

He heard a mighty rushing, as of the wind, as the balustrade snapped and its rail slipped forward. For a moment, it was an intermittent thing, similar to the flapping sound of a garment hung out to dry.

As he was cast over the edge, he was able to turn and look upward.

Falling, he saw a dark figure in the sky that grew even as his eyes passed over it.

Of course, he thought, he has finally looked upon the sunrise and been freed . . .

Wings folded, his great, horned countenance impassive, Morningstar dropped like a black meteor. As he drew near, he extended his arms full length and opened his massive hands.

Jack wondered whether he would arrive in time.

ABOUT THE AUTHOR

ROGER ZELAZNY is an expatriate Ohioan who now resides on a mountaintop in New Mexico with his wife, Judy; sons Devin and Trent; daughter, Shannon; assorted typewriters, oriental rugs, unanswered letters, and science fiction awards. The awards, which he keeps close on hand in his office—"Never can tell when you might need one in a hurry"—consist of three Hugos, three Nebulas, a Balrog, and the mystical presence of the Prix Apollo. He has had 26 books published, and his works have been translated into 14 foreign languages, transcribed in Braille, and done as Talking Books. One of his novels was made into a movie, and another has been sold for the same purpose. He is currently working on a new novel. Also available in Signet editions are Roger Zelazny's fine novels, *Today We Choose Faces* and *Bridge of Ashes*.